Lilly's Ransom

Lilly's Ransom

Ensley Williams

Aventine Press

Published by Aventine Press
1023 4th Ave #204
San Diego CA, 92101
www.aventinepress.com

ISBN: 1-59330-358-0

Library of Congress Control Number: 2005929767

For Fay Myers Williams

ransom n. 1. the freeing of a captive or of seized property by payment of money or fulfillment of other demands 2. the price thus paid 3. freedom from sin, redemption

Prologue

Lilly cupped her hands under the spout of the rusty iron pitcher pump and caught the cool water surging up from the Florida limestone deep beneath her. She splashed her hot face and neck, and then her arms, the water soaking through her cotton dress and dripping down to the pine boards of the porch floor. The wide, over-hanging roof above her was a blessing, helping to calm the blazing afternoon sun. Lilly had been in Florida for more than half of her twenty-three years, but she still hated the sun—hated its constant assault upon her skin.

Everybody thought Lilly was beautiful. She was like her mother—had the same soft face, the dark brown hair and eyes, and pretty hands. She also had, although somewhat faded, the voice and manners of the polite Savannah society into which she was born. But a gentle birth doesn't bring a heart that is always gentle and patient. Maybe it was the blood of her fiery Welsh ancestors. It didn't just flow through her veins; sometimes it boiled. And now it was about to boil over.

"I could kill him now," she said out loud to herself. "I could kill him today, and nobody would blame me."

Anger always took a physical toll on Lilly. She felt the familiar stuttering heartbeat, the sinking feeling in her chest, and then the palpitations. Slumping down into the porch swing, she held the chain with one hand, and placing her other hand over her eyes, laid her head against the armrest and tried to breathe deeply. In a little while, she began feeling better, and for a moment, the world became a kinder place. She parted her fingers and watched the leaves and fruit of the Surinam cherry bush beginning to stir in the soft gulf breeze.

The peace was broken by the rattling motor of a Model T Ford turning in at the gate. Lilly sat up and watched as her best friend, Grace Morgan, steered through the powdery, white sand of the long driveway. Grace parked under the shade of the huge eucalyptus tree, and with her usual energy, kicked open the car door, sprang from the running board, and ran toward the house.

"My God, Lilly, you're soaked!" she called out in surprise. "Did you fall in the lake?"

"The bastard really did it this time, Grace. You can read the letter yourself; it's on the kitchen table."

Grace's shoulders sagged. She let out a long sigh and bit her lip. "Honey, all of this is gonna kill you. Little-by-little, maybe, but it's gonna kill you."

"Grace, somebody's going to get killed, but it won't be me, and it won't be little-by-little. I may just take the shotgun and..."

Lilly pressed her lips together as hard as she could. It was something she always did when she thought she was going to cry. The tears came anyway. She looked at her friend and tried to control her breaking voice. "Sometimes I think Mama and Papa should have just stayed in Savannah."

Chapter 1

Elizabeth Jenkins and her husband were anxious to leave Savannah in 1908. Their families had been in Georgia for three generations, but it was time for a new life. Too many people there were still looking back, longing for the cotton and rice empire their fathers had fought for and lost. Elizabeth wanted to tell them they could never have it again—anymore than the old veterans could have their missing arms and legs. Reconstruction had been replaced by the Gilded Age, but it seemed Savannah had been left behind—like a tattered but elegant ball gown exiled in a musty closet.

It wasn't hard to convince Judge Jenkins. He felt it was probably time for another major change in his life. As a young man, he had been a good trial lawyer, and in so much demand that he had remained a bachelor for too long. But it had been twelve years now since Elizabeth had given him a reason to settle down, and a reason to take a place on the Chatham County bench. His brother and youngest sister had already left Savannah with their children years earlier, and now that he was raising a family of his own, he decided it would be good for *his* children to have a new adventure, too. He kissed his spinster sister goodbye, knowing that she would never leave Savannah. Then, with eleven-year-old Lilly and eight-year-old Evan, he and Elizabeth came to the west coast of Florida, to a rambling white house nestled among the pine trees and live oaks north of Tampa Bay. In an idyllic childhood perfumed with orange blossoms and jasmine, Lilly and Evan caught sunfish from the shimmering lake, listened to whippoorwills at night, and waited for the humming birds that hovered above the hibiscus outside the kitchen window.

The Jenkinses were not, however, country people at heart. Judge Jenkins joined a law firm in Tampa and made the daily trips to town. The city was booming. Northerners were coming to work, or to invest, in the seaport, and the cigar factories in Ybor City and West Tampa were filling with Cuban and Sicilian immigrants. Lilly came into town with her father at every chance to visit her cousins or to shop in the stores with her mother, but nights in the country were lonely. And then she met Grace.

It was at a cousin's birthday party in town. Lilly was fascinated with the smiling blonde whose blue eyes looked straight into hers, and who was so ready to know everything about her and talk about everything. They became almost inseparable from the start. Dr. and Mrs. Morgan's big two-story house in the heart of town became like a second home for Lilly.

The girls spent hours in Grace's bedroom overlooking the streetcar line. They watched the world below them changing as the years rolled on toward 1918 and the end of the Great War. Ragtime became jazz, and Gibson Girls began to disappear.

Like all young women, Lilly and Grace talked mostly about young men. One afternoon, there was a particular young man who caught their attention. The streetcars were filled with soldiers returning from Europe, and the girls waved immodestly from Grace's window. A tall, good-looking captain, who was just then stepping down from the trolley, waved back. Even from the second-floor window, it seemed he was looking at Lilly.

The marriage was held on a Sunday morning. Judge Jenkins was giving his daughter to a man who knew what he wanted. Captain McKinley Harrison wanted to be out of the army, and he wanted to be rich. Somewhere in his mind, he also had a picture of the kind of woman he wanted with him. Lilly seemed ideal: beautiful, amiable, and sweet. During their short engagement, he caught glimpses of her underlying strength and occasional fire, but it was of no great concern. Women, he believed, only needed to be given material comforts, and perhaps an occasional luxury, to purchase their obedience. He felt they were morally weak, and he was sure that they lacked the character of the men he had led in battle.

Something had changed Mac Harrison. Something had turned his attention inward. The horrors of the Argonne Forest had had an effect on all the young men who had gone "over there" with so much pride and ambition. Lives were wasted and sacrificed on an enormous scale, and almost everyone who made it—who crossed the Meuse River—came back a changed man. Some changed for the best, and found a way to think about all they had seen. But Mac thought only about himself. Everyone around him would now occupy a subordinate position, and because of his charm, would spend their energy (and whatever affection they felt) in keeping him happy.

Lilly didn't see this in the man she was marrying. She had no experience on which to base such a judgment, and she was not fully aware that a man could be so fundamentally different from the ones already in her life. Her father was a strong, intelligent man who succeeded in both his family and the world at large without guile or dishonesty. Evan would be like him, she thought, or perhaps like her mother, which wouldn't be a bad thing at all.

Grace would see less of her best friend, but she wanted her to be happy. She purposely stayed away—more than she would have liked—to give Lilly time to get to know her husband. As time passed, Lilly found it harder to talk, even though Grace would have been ready to listen.

The signs came slowly. The living arrangements of the new couple kept Mac Harrison from assuming full command of what he considered his new post. It was decided that they would live, at least for a time, with her family so that Mac could be closer to the sawmill that he had been hired to manage. Mac had impressed the owner with his military credentials. Impressing Lilly's mother was a much harder thing to do.

Mac knew which side of himself to show to Lilly's father, but Elizabeth's intuitive good sense and constant presence were obstacles he couldn't overcome. Of all of the people close to Lilly, she would have been the one quickest to see trouble looming, and the one most capable of protecting her.

Elizabeth Jenkins was an incredibly strong and forceful woman, but there had been scarlet fever in her childhood, and in its aftermath, a damaged heart. On a beautiful, bright winter morning, Judge Jenkins tried to wake her to see the frost on the lawn—one of the things about Georgia she missed most. He had tried to prepare himself for years for this day; now all he could think of was how beautiful and peaceful she looked, and how Lilly and Evan were going to miss her. As for himself, he couldn't bear the thought of being in the house without her—he would see her at every turn—so he left to stay with his sister in town, confident that Lilly would have a joyous life in the house she grew up in, loved and protected by her handsome husband.

Two years after her marriage, Lilly was living alone in the empty house, and on this day, looking out through the kitchen window at her mother's garden while Grace sat at the table behind her and read, in disbelief, the letter from Mac Harrison.

New Orleans
July 21, 1921
My Dearest Lil:

I know you must be worried by now, but I have been constantly on the move since last week. I haven't quite known what to say to you at any rate, but I must tell you not to do anything that will harm me, or I should say, harm both of us. First of all, do not try to draw money from the bank. I have written a very large draft against it that must be honored. The man holding it is not a person to trifle with. It is almost all of the money we have. Please, dearest, do not try to involve Evan in this; he is young and has no experience with a business like this.

Lil, if you only knew how much I care for you and love you, you would understand why I have done all of the things I have done in these past months—it has all been only for you, and for our happiness. Please do nothing until you hear from me again. Talk to no one about this.

Your Loving Husband

P.S. My Dear Girl, please do not tell anyone where I am, and do not show this letter to Grace. I know that I can trust you in this.

A faint, bitter smile crossed Grace's lips as she read the last line. This is just like Mac, she thought—too confident for his own good and always believing he is in control of everyone—whether he is around or not. Grace put down the letter, got up from the table and placed her hands on Lilly's shoulders. "Honey, how much money did you have in the bank?" she asked. "You don't have to tell me if you don't want to; I'm just trying to fathom all of this."

"I don't mind telling you, Grace. There was over twenty-thousand dollars there last week. God knows where it is now. I talked to Mr. Lassiter at the bank after Mac had been gone for two days. By then I had figured out that he wasn't coming back right away. Most of that money was from Papa. It was more than he should have given us, but you know how he is. It was not supposed to be used for Mac's business speculations, especially not the kind he has been engaged in lately. I let him borrow some for a day or two. He always put it back. I should never have done that; I should have insisted that he use the other money he had, but apparently he was running out of that."

"Does Mr. Lassiter know anything about this?"

"I really don't have any idea what he knows. I only told him that Mac had left, and I wanted to make sure he hadn't taken a lot of money with him."

"But, Lilly, surely Mac hasn't been able to keep everyone from knowing. Mr. Lassiter must be curious about the way Mac comes and goes with all this money. You can't run a bank in a town like Tampa and not be on to these things."

Lilly sat down at the table and read the letter for the tenth time while Grace paced back and forth in the kitchen. The room looked just as it did when Judge and Mrs. Jenkins had lived there. Grace was thinking about Lilly's father now and about the way his daughter was hiding her life from him. "Lilly, you know I haven't tried to interfere with the way you've handled this," she said, trying to look away as she spoke, "but I think it's time you told your papa. He's so smart. He would know exactly the thing to do. He always does. That's one of the reasons everyone admires him so much."

"But, Grace, that's just it—he would be so embarrassed about this. Papa has built such a reputation in Tampa. Everybody calls him Judge—just like in Savannah. As long as I can keep him from knowing, I will. And I didn't write Evan—not to please Mac, but he's right."

Grace had been hiding something, herself. She stood behind Lilly's chair, closed her eyes, and took a deep breath. "Honey, I don't think it will be much longer before he finds out. There's something I need to tell you. I was in Ybor City yesterday, and Nick Cancello saw me in the Americana Restaurant. He took me by the arm and just about dragged me out the back door to talk. You know, I really don't think Nick's a bad guy at all; when he took me dancing at the pier on Valentine's Day, he was a perfect gentleman."

"Grace, what on earth does this have to do with anything?" Lilly asked, turning around in her chair, and then turning back again while her friend gathered her courage.

"Honey, Nick knows the guys Mac has been dealing with, and he knows Mac owes them a lot of money. He wanted to warn me about something. He said Ivan Moss asked him if your papa had a lot of money."

Obvious pain flashed across Lilly's face. For almost a minute, she sat in stunned silence. She got up from the table with her back still turned to Grace. "Do you still keep that bottle of gin in the car?" she asked, looking up and sighing.

"It's there, just like always. Are we taking a ride?"

Grace waited in a white wicker chair on the long front veranda while Lilly dressed and got a few things together. They would drive into town and stay at Grace's. There would be time to talk about what they would say to Lilly's father.

After Lilly dressed, she sat with her friend for a few minutes to clear her head and to cool off from the exertion of packing her clothes. "Will your mama wonder why I've come home with you?" she asked. "You know, I've never done that since I've been married."

"I don't think so, Lilly. She always loves to see you. Papa is still in Plant City with a patient, so he won't be back tonight. Mama is always up early like you, and she'll enjoy the company. I suppose you want to drive again."

The Model T was Grace's most prized possession. It was like a pair of wings for her. There were plenty of men in town who would have stood in line to drive the pretty, petite, blonde Miss Morgan anywhere she cared to go, but Grace's sense of independence extended further than her flapper clothes. She wasn't about to be hauled around like a chicken in a crate—not by anybody. Now, however, she would allow her best friend to get behind the wheel. It was obvious that Lilly was in no mood to sit still.

Grace bent down in front of the car and turned the crank. After two or three tries, a sharp bang, and a puff of smoke, the engine came to life. Grace then retrieved the bottle of smuggled English gin from its hiding place behind the back seat. "At least this is the good stuff," she said smiling, trying to recapture any small remnant of the good times they used to have.

"Anything would be better than that awful poison you made for New Year's Eve. I don't know why you just don't let the fellas get it for you all the time; it's really not that hard anymore. Anyway, let's wait till we get to town to have a drink. We can park by the bay for a while. I think your mama has finally stopped trying to catch liquor on our breath these days. You know, in a way, it makes me feel old."

Lilly and Grace were naturally good-natured. Their light, teasing humor still came through even in bad times, and even in a crowd, they could be uncannily in tune with each other. The two years of Lilly's marriage had not really changed this. As she shut the car door, Lilly glanced at her friend and saw again the energy that she had first been drawn to seven years ago. Something told her that her life would be different now.

The cypress trees to the west were throwing long shadows across the front lawn and driveway as Lilly maneuvered the car through the gate and out onto the rutted country road. The two young women were silent for a moment, each having different thoughts about the coming meeting with Lilly's father. The Ford engine made a steady clatter, and the springs groaned at each rough spot in the road as they made their way through the pine and palmetto scrublands toward Tampa. The only other sounds, other than an occasional passing vehicle, were Lilly's heavy sighs as she gripped the steering wheel and tried to cope with the winding turns and the setting sun.

Chapter 2

It was dark when Lilly parked the car under a tall sabal palm on the shore of Hillsborough Bay. The scorching afternoon had given way to a humid evening, and the heavy, muggy air had turned the water to a flat, glassy calm. Far out in the distance, though, the usual tall clouds of summer were turning black and rumbling across the bay. Soon, cool, misty air billowed through the open windows of the car, and thin drops of rain blew against the windshield.

"Let's leave the windows open as long as we can," said Lilly. "This is the first time all day I haven't been roasting." She leaned back against the door and tried to gather her thoughts while Grace opened the gin and tried to talk Lilly into a happier state of mind.

"We're just gonna have to drink it from the bottle, honey—not too fancy, I'm afraid."

"Apparently, I'll have to get used to not being fancy, Gracie. You know, Mama and Papa were never what I would call rich, but I don't think they ever had to worry about money, so I've never worried about it either."

Grace took a not-too-small sip and handed the bottle to her friend. Lilly put it to her lips, swallowed hard, and shook her head. She was not much accustomed to straight liquor, but she held on to the bottle for the time being.

Alcohol acts on people in mysterious ways. It can stimulate some to homicidal rages, and it can depress others into maudlin stupors. It can be giddy and gay or melancholy and silent. In Lilly—at least on this night— it seemed to make her see many things more clearly, and helped her to chart out the course that she would follow. She would start by not thinking of herself as Mrs. Harrison anymore—she was her father's daughter. He had always protected her, but now she might have to protect him as well.

"Gracie, there are a lot of things I need to find out, but what I'm most worried about is this idea that someone would try to get money from Papa. If Mac has used all that we have in the bank, I think we're in trouble. I also have a feeling that he owes these people a lot more."

The wind began to blow in heavy gusts, and sharp cracks of thunder caused them to close up the car as rain and small hail pelted down in a deafening barrage. Lilly talked on above the noise, her tongue and inhibitions loosened by the liquor. She talked of the doubts that had come early in her marriage, and how she had concealed them from everyone. She tried to explain her uncharacteristic submission to her husband's subtle tyranny. She hadn't started out that way, but grief over her mother's death may have softened her, she said; and maybe she had tried too hard to be good, to be a proper and helpful wife.

Grace looked out toward the bay as the moon broke through the thinning rain clouds and illuminated the tops of the rippling waves. She tried to think of a way to ease her friend's fears. "Lilly, what do you think those people can really do?" she asked. "It's not a legitimate debt, I'm sure."

"I believe those people can do whatever they want, Grace. The first thing I have to find out is how much Mac is into them for. I need to forget everything he's told me and try to get to the truth some other way. If it's not too late, I need to take the money out of the bank, or at least make sure it's safe. I don't know what to make of the letter; Mac has never written a check to anyone before. He's always kept a lot of cash at the house. I think he had gone through most of it right before he left—and he left so suddenly. He hardly said a word; he just put his suitcase in the Packard and drove off. That was on a Saturday night; he wouldn't have been able to get any cash from the bank. Grace, I think I can deal with Mac, but I can't let anybody hurt Papa. He's fifty-six years old now. He's getting to the age where he shouldn't have to worry about anything, and he needs to stop working so hard. I'm through with Mac; if Papa wants to come back home, that would be fine with me."

It was almost ten o'clock when Grace and Lilly pulled under the porte-cocheres of the Morgans' house. Mrs. Morgan met them at the door and kissed Lilly. Almost immediately—because of fatigue, because of fear, because the gin weakened her defenses—Lilly began to cry. She fell onto the sofa, buried her face in her folded arms, and sobbed. Grace knelt at her friend's side and stroked her hair while her mother went for a cool washcloth.

When she returned, Mrs. Morgan placed the cloth over Lilly's swollen eyes. She knew the young woman well enough to know that she was not weak, and she wondered at the cause of so much grief.

"Please, dear, try to tell me about it," she began. "There is nothing that we wouldn't help you with. If it's something that you need Dr. Morgan for, he will be home tomorrow."

Grace spoke for her. "Mama, it's really awful. Mac's been gone for over a week, and he's in a lot of trouble. He owes people, some really bad people, a lot of money, and it looks like the cad's giving away all that's left."

"Now, Grace, don't talk in such a fashion; Mr. Harrison is her husband. You must understand that things like this always pass, but whatever you say will be remembered."

"But he's not my husband now," Lilly said, wiping her eyes as she sat up. "I'm going to see Papa in the morning, but I can tell you everything—if you can bear to hear it."

"Certainly I can bear it, dear, if you want to tell me, but be careful about anything that may embarrass you later. Everything may not be as it appears, and you may have a change of heart."

"I'm not sure that I have a heart anymore," Lilly said, as she lifted the damp strands of hair away from her face and tried again to dry her eyes. "Not for him, anyway. I've had a lot of time to think because I've been alone a lot in the last few months. Everybody thinks Mac has been working late at the sawmill office, but that's not true.

The sawmill is probably going to be closed anyway; the owner went back to Connecticut. Mac started spending a lot of time at the docks when he went down to handle the shipments of lumber going out. He got hooked up with Frank Moss's son, Ivan, and—"

"Oh my word, Lilly! Frank Moss is just an awful man; doesn't Mac know that?"

"Not at all, Mrs. Morgan. Mac thinks Mr. Moss is the only person in Florida with any style. Right before Christmas, he started dressing just like him and his son— you know, the fancy shoes and everything. The thing is, he got into business with them. He said they were going to import birds—parrots and such—that come up to Mexico from South America."

Grace's mother was bewildered. "Dear, do you mean to tell me that Mr. Harrison would give up such a promising career in the lumber business just to sell ornamental birds at the docks?"

"Tropical birds, Mama," said Grace, rolling her eyes.

"Well it's not exactly like that, you see," Lilly continued. "The birds would have been sent to New York then. But it appears that there was something else going on. They were bringing in a few birds, but it was something hidden in the shipments with them that they were really after. Apparently, there are a great many people up north who are taking laudanum and morphine."

"Prostitutes mostly," said Grace, who was so glad that Lilly was finally uncovering her secret that she wanted to help tell the story. "There are hundreds of prostitutes in New York, and they all drug themselves terribly."

"Oh my Lord Jesus, girls! What a thing to be involved in! How long have you known about this, Lilly?"

"Since right after Christmas. Mac had been up north for two weeks; he came in on the train on Christmas Eve. He told me to meet him at Union Station, but to come alone. I had a terrible time trying to explain to Papa and Evan. They wanted to drive me there, but I was able to use Aunt Maggie's Oldsmobile. As soon as Mac got off the train, he gave me my Christmas gift. It was an incredibly expensive diamond and ruby necklace. I had helped Uncle Oliver with his store quite often, so I know the value of jewelry. I kept it for a time, but I wouldn't wear it, of course. Anyone with any sense would surely have thought it odd. Mac has a bit of money from his family, and he certainly has been well paid by the mill owners, but he doesn't—or shouldn't—have the money for that kind of thing."

Mrs. Morgan's sense of astonishment grew. From the moment of the girls' arrival, this had been an incredible evening; she hardly knew what question to ask. "Well, where is it now, dear?"

"He finally took it back. As it turns out, he would have eventually had to, anyway. All this business has been chaotic, to say the least. He would have a pocketful of money on one day, and then be drawing from the bank on the next. But I finally got most of the truth from him—oh, I guess sometime last month. He was in real trouble by then, and he admitted everything about the laudanum. It seems he has been dealing with people who are stealing from Mr. Moss, and it seems to have all caught up with him. He left in such a hurry that I believe someone, perhaps Ivan Moss, is after him."

Grace could keep silent no longer. "Mama, Lilly may lose everything. According to Nick Cancello, these men may even try to get money from Judge Jenkins."

"Please don't tell me you're seeing that man again, Grace. I know you are no longer a child, and I can't hover over you as though you were, but you will never meet a respectable man when you are seen with people like that. The war is over now, and people are settling down and raising families."

"Mama, don't worry about me; I'm not the one who needs tending."

"Well, certainly, you're right, Grace. I wish your father were home; I've never had to cope with such a case as this. At any rate, I believe the proper thing is for Lilly to inform her father right away. Lilly, you really cannot endure this alone. I've always thought of you as a bright, sensible, young lady, but a woman is no match for these types. I just find it unthinkable that your husband has brought you to this."

Lilly felt a sense of relief at the disclosure of her troubles, but the experience had left her drained. After accepting Mrs. Morgan's offer of a glass of milk, she leaned her head against the back of the sofa and asked to be left alone for a while in the darkened room. The last traces of the gin were wearing off, leaving her feeling somewhat dull and empty. Sleep would clear her mind and help her face her father tomorrow. She wearily climbed the stairs to Grace's familiar room and undressed quietly, without waking her friend.

Warm air rising from the street below was lifting the curtains in the open window. Without really trying, Lilly could see the deserted trolley stand under the yellow street light. For the third time today, she pressed her lips together hard. This time she didn't cry.

Chapter 3

Five hundred miles to the northwest of Tampa Bay, across the Gulf of Mexico, and up the winding course of the Mississippi River, lies the city of New Orleans. All kinds of people had passed through the old city in the two-hundred years between 1721 and 1921: explorers with royal commissions, bankers and merchants looking for new ways to make money, and gamblers, thieves, and harlots who just wanted a new place to ply their ancient occupations. Some came to build new countries, some were escaping old countries, and others were escaping enemies, both old and new.

Hiding from enemies requires resourcefulness and planning, and the building of new liaisons. Mac Harrison knew this almost instinctively. For most of the night, he had been deep in thought, sitting up in bed in a small French Quarter hotel. There was little thought about the wife who he had left in Florida, and who was now sleeping with an unburdened heart in the care of people who loved her. As far as he was concerned, she should not be a problem. She would do as she was told in the letter and keep everything to herself. In the meantime, he would make use of people here.

He would need help in dealing with Frank Moss. It was going to be much harder than he first thought, and perhaps he had been overconfident. The war had made him courageous, but also a little reckless. In the beginning, it had seemed easy. The Moss family had generally left him alone, left him free to operate at his own discretion. He had brought in plenty of money—enough to cause them to trust him with more. Now, as it always had been, money was also a problem.

For the past three days, Mac had been looking for Henry Wasson. He had last seen the man in New York, where they had had a hurried exchange of money and merchandise at a late night meeting in Battery Park. The two men had been arms-length partners in a small side operation, taking portions of the drug shipments and sending them south again to Henry's address in New Orleans. The risks were greater there, but the profits were higher; the drugs could be diluted and sold to the users directly. There was more than enough to enrich Mac and Henry and still give Ivan Moss his expected return. Mac's cut of the money was long overdue, however. Henry had promised to have the money ready and to bring it to Tampa by the end of June.

By the middle of July, all of Mac's problems were coming to a head, and the intricate lies and deceptions were unraveling. The Moss family had finally lost patience. Although they had far more money than that which was tied up in Mac's scheme, they weren't in the habit of losing any of it. They had built their small empire on a reputation of ruthlessness; there could be no sign of weakness displayed on any front.

Mac could not allow himself to go to sleep until he had a new plan for tomorrow. Since arriving in town, he had accomplished nothing. The address Wasson had given him had turned out to be an empty warehouse. If anyone around the place knew where to find the man, they were not saying.

Mac tried to concentrate on the things that he did know. For one thing, Henry Wasson should have plenty of money on him. If that was still true, he would be spending lots of it, and he would be spending it on the things he liked most.

There were a lot of women in New Orleans. Most of them wouldn't be all that interested in Henry Wasson, but some of them would be interested in what he had to offer. It suddenly occurred to Mac that he could do what he had done during the war. He had been very good at using captured German soldiers to lead him to an objective. It would take a little time, but he would find someone to lead him to what was left of his money. He could use a little company, he decided; it had been over two weeks since he had last been with Lilly.

For now, Mac needed sleep. He got up from the bed and took a small bottle of morphine from his suitcase.

At ten o'clock the next morning, Mac was sitting in a cool bath at the end of the hallway. Most of the other guests on his floor had awakened earlier and had gone on their way; he would have the bathroom to himself for a while. He rolled a cigarette with damp fingers and struck the match on the rough wall behind him. The cool water was just what he needed after the hot, sticky night. He would spend a little money later on a haircut and shave. It was time, he thought, to be confident and forceful again, the way he had always been.

There was still the matter of the bank draft he had written. It was, indeed, made out to a man not to be trifled with: Mr. McKinley Harrison. There was a banker he knew in Birmingham—Major Selwyn from his infantry company—who should cash it without question. He had counted on Lilly being naive enough to believe that he would actually write a check to someone he was involved with in the narcotics trade. He would use the money to start a new life. It was little more than half of the money that he owed to Frank Moss, anyway. If he couldn't find Wasson and recover the full amount, he would be better off to take what he could and run. There would be no going back after that. Deceivers know better than anyone else that deceit has its limits. Mac took a deep drag on the short nub of his cigarette and talked out-loud to himself. "Well, if I do have to disappear for good, she'll have to get herself out of this. She didn't want what I could give her, but I bet she doesn't mind taking more from that old man. He'll spend everything he's got to keep from even smelling Ivan Moss."

Mac dressed in the best of the three light suits he had brought with him and ate breakfast in a small coffee house on Royal Street. He wanted to forget Tampa for a while, but the *cafe au lait* reminded him too much of the *cafe con leche* he had become accustomed to in Ybor City. Just before noon, he walked up Canal Street and looked for a barber shop near one of the larger hotels.

While he waited for an empty chair, Mac listened to the constant chatter of the barbers and customers in the shop. Barbers are the same everywhere, he thought; they're more gossipy than women. This would be as good a source of information as anyplace in New Orleans. When his turn in the chair came, Mac wasted no time in opening a conversation.

"Tell me, Joe, you been a barber in New Orleans very long?"

"Long as I been grown, Mister. Daddy started this shop and gave it to us kids—course we ain't exactly kids no more—that's my brother Gus down there."

"I'm looking for an old friend. I wonder if you might know him."

"Old friend that owes you, I bet."

"His name is Henry Wasson. I would really like to see him again."

"I may know some Wassons, Mister, but I can't really say I know a Henry. Even if I did, I might be a little hard pressed to tell you about it—gotta be a little shy about stuff like that in this town, if you know what I mean."

Mac could see that this was a dead-end street, so he decided to change course. "Well, you're not shy about telling a guy where to find some company, are you?"

"No need in tellin' anybody 'bout that—a man can't find a woman for hisself in New Orleans, can't find one nowhere—no offense now, Mister. They may call it Bourbon Street, but it oughta be called *Putain* Street—if you know what I mean. You know, I'm just havin' fun with you, Mister, but really, a well-turned-out gentleman like yourself should look for company in the hotels—the nice hotels, anyhow."

After his shave, Mac paid the barber and added a generous tip. If he was going to be here for a time, he reasoned, it would be best to start making friends. The next step would be to find a better hotel. There was no reason to believe that anyone except Lilly knew of his whereabouts, so it should be just as safe in more luxurious surroundings.

As Mac closed the door of the barbershop behind him, the two brothers inside looked at each other with raised brows. "Joe, you gonna call Henry and tell him that boy's lookin' to find him?"

"I ain't callin' nobody, Gus—at least not right now. Maybe things get worrisome, it'll be a different story. Nobody knows where Henry is most of the time, anyhow. And damn, Gus, Henry's got money—he can take care of hisself."

Chapter 4

All of her life, Lilly had been an early riser. Whenever she had slept at Grace's, she had always gotten up before sunrise, when the stars and planets were clear and bright against the black sky. She would stand at the window, while her friend was still asleep, and wait for the first rays of dawn to shine their light on the silver minarets of the Tampa Bay Hotel.

On this day, however, she was awakened by the bright mid-morning sun and the presence of someone sitting at the foot of her bed. It was her papa.

"Sugar, Mrs. Morgan has breakfast ready," he said softly. "You need to get dressed and come down. I've already had a talk with Grace. She came to the office to get me as soon as I came in this morning. After you've had something to eat, we'll talk a little more, and then we need to go to the bank. I gave a call to Mr. Lassiter, so he's expecting us."

"I feel like I've been sleeping forever, Papa. Grace told you everything?"

"Yes, sugar, I think she did, but you just come downstairs now. I'm sure you're hungry."

Judge Jenkins lightly patted his daughter's ankle as he got up from the bed, the way he used to do when she was a little girl, and left the room. He had always been this way, Lilly thought: calm and in charge of the situation. She wished that she had confided in him sooner, before things had gotten this far.

Grace sat at the table with Lilly and had another cup of coffee while her friend tried to wipe the sleep from her eyes. Lilly wasn't really very hungry, but she tried to eat the eggs and bacon that were set before her.

"Gracie, I didn't really drink too much of the gin last night, did I?" she asked meekly. "I don't feel very well."

"I don't think so, honey; you don't ever drink too much, as far as I know."

While the young women remained in the kitchen, Judge Jenkins and Mrs. Morgan talked quietly in the adjacent dining room. "Judge, there is one thing I am really worried about," the woman began sternly. "It seems that Grace has been seeing a set of people that includes those Cancello boys. I know that she is very close to Lilly, but I really don't want her mixed up with the kind of people with which Mr. Harrison associates."

"Mrs. Morgan, I don't think you have much of a worry on that point. Grace told me what Nick Cancello said to her. The thing is, I know that family quite well, and they are not so bad as you might think. Nick is the youngest son, but he has settled down quite a bit. He was in a bit of a scrape a few years ago, and our firm got him out of it. I've talked to him several times lately;

he has made a good impression. He can't help who he knows. The fact is, I am thinking of looking him up this afternoon."

"Judge, surely you have no good opinion of Frank Moss."

"He is another matter entirely, and I want to leave him alone for the time being. But Nick Cancello will tell me what he knows. It's apparent that he was trying to be helpful by the warning he gave to Grace. I'm really grateful to her for telling Lilly about it right away."

"Don't you think, Judge, that you should inform the police chief about all of this?"

Lilly's father had always liked Mrs. Morgan, but he sometimes grew impatient with her obtuseness. His face reddened at her last remark, but he measured his words carefully. "I absolutely do not, and I'm sure I can trust you to keep this matter to yourself. I suppose you can tell Dr. Morgan about it. After all, I would like Lilly to stay here, if that is no great imposition. You must understand, though, that Lilly could be found to be somewhat culpable herself, if the police department or the sheriff gets involved. She knew all about these dealings, it seems. I certainly don't want to upset her now, but at some point, I want to know why she acquiesced in this."

In spite of the hot weather, Lilly agreed to walk with her father across the Lafayette Street Bridge to the bank downtown. Before they were half-way across, Judge Jenkins was sorry that he had suggested the walk. It was apparent that his daughter was sick. But Lilly knew that all of this had to be done, and she was sure that her father must be disappointed in her.

By the time they reached the Peninsula National Bank, Lilly's nausea had subsided, and more importantly, she had fully regained her determination. For the last three years, she had given up control of her life to a man who couldn't control his own. Starting today, she decided, she would do whatever was necessary to get hers back again.

Raymond Lassiter was waiting at his desk for Judge Jenkins. The busy bank vice president liked the courtly, soft-spoken Georgian, but he didn't have a good feeling about the nature of the visit. He was becoming increasingly concerned with Mac Harrison's account. It fluctuated wildly, and he suspected that Lilly was unaware of the many hurried withdrawals. These were always followed by large cash deposits in order to bring the balance back up to the amount she would expect to find whenever she made a visit. He also knew that Mac always picked up the written statements as soon as they were prepared.

Lilly's last visit to the bank had unnerved him, though; he could only inform her of the balance as of that day. He was also somewhat surprised by her indiscreet admission that her husband had left town suddenly, and that she had no idea of his whereabouts.

As Lilly and her father came in to the banker's office, he rose and greeted them. "Good morning, Judge; it's always good to see you, sir. Good to see you, Mrs. Harrison."

Both men were startled when Lilly answered first. "Let's get right to the matter, Mr. Lassiter. Do I have any money left in this bank?"

Mr. Lassiter smiled and regained his bearing. "Yes, ma'am, you do. As of this morning you have the same amount as last week. Let me see here—yes—it looks like twenty-three thousand, six-hundred and forty-two dollars—and some change, of course."

The judge spoke up quickly. "That is what we wanted to hear, sir. I think it's best that my daughter withdraw that money this morning."

"My goodness, folks, I don't see any reason for anything like that. It doesn't appear that there is anything irregular about the account; it's had no activity for more than a week."

"That doesn't mean anything," Lilly said forcefully. "I've heard from Mr. Harrison. I received a letter from him yesterday. It seems he's written a draft for almost all of it, and I don't even know to whom."

"Well, that's somewhat of a problem, Mrs. Harrison. If that is true, and you don't leave enough to cover it, the holder would almost certainly report it for prosecution, especially with an amount of that size—not to mention the fact that the bank also takes a very dim view of worthless instruments."

"Papa, I suppose I should let you answer that."

"I was about to do that, sugar. Mr. Lassiter, there is a reason why I'm here with my daughter. Ordinarily, I would let her and Mr. Harrison manage their own affairs, but first of all, it seems he is out of the picture now. More importantly, most of the money in that account was a wedding gift from Lilly's mother and me. There is no person, to my knowledge at least, who would be the legitimate recipient of such a check. Now, Raymond, I believe you and I have come to be good friends. I want you to forget about what Lilly just told you about the letter. She spoke without thinking. She hasn't been feeling very well today, and I think she's a little confused. Let's just say that she wants to make a withdrawal. She certainly has every right to do that."

There was not another word spoken. Lilly and her father sat quietly while Mr. Lassiter took care of the necessary paperwork. Then, in his quiet, almost regal manner, Judge Jenkins escorted his daughter across the bank lobby and out into the summer heat. Lilly held tightly to her purse. It contained her wedding gift of two years ago—a gift given with no expectation of any return other than her own happiness.

Chapter 5

Ivan Moss sat alone in the Tropic Cafe and tried to swallow his lunch. Nothing was going down. He had given up on the Cuban sandwich, but even the garbanzo bean soup was hard to take. His father had screamed at him for what seemed like an hour, and nobody could scream like Frank Moss. It seemed to Ivan that he would never be treated like a man. He was twenty-six now, and should have some level of respect. But this thing, he thought, was probably his own fault; he had been too damned lazy to keep track of Mac Harrison.

Ivan had all of the gifts necessary to operate his father's business interests. He was over six-feet tall, and had been a champion prizefighter until his father had lost patience with such unproductive work. Since that time, he had done everything he had been told to do. He found a woman to marry and moved into the house his father had bought for them. He wasn't a brilliant man, but he was smart enough to figure out the best ways to make money in this business. It wasn't really all that hard for him—

there was money everywhere. People hated Prohibition, and they didn't mind paying for good liquor.

The drugs were more interesting, though. He always said that any cracker could find rum or moonshine to sell. The narcotics business was growing, and it involved a lot of traveling. It gave him a chance to be on his own. Everything was going well, he thought, except for this problem with Harrison. Mac's operation was not a huge part of the drug money, but Ivan liked the man because he was smarter than most of the others. Mac was a good-looking guy, he thought, somebody good to go on the stag with. Ugly guys were bad to be seen with when girls were around, no matter how much loot you had to spend.

Ivan was sorry that all the good times were over. It didn't make sense. Mac Harrison should have been a safe bet because of his wife. It didn't seem likely that he would run out on the daughter of a rich, downtown lawyer. But it seemed less likely that he would be stupid enough to steal from the family. His father wouldn't care about all that, though. Frank Moss didn't waste time trying to analyze people—he had had enough of this. It was time to find Harrison and take back the money. If he didn't have it, somebody else would have to pay.

Six blocks away from the Tropic, Lilly's father and Grace were just sitting down to lunch with Nick Cancello. The judge appeared out-of-season but still well dressed in a dark tailored suit of pre-war design. Grace, on the other hand, looked modern and kinetic, her waistline fashionably lower and her hem daringly higher than those of the older women in the room. Her purple cloche hat, pulled down snugly just above her eyebrows, did not entirely obscure her cropped, bright hair.

Nick, who could never look at Grace without smiling, was the youngest son of a Sicilian immigrant family. They had come, like many others, from Santo Stefano to work in the cigar factories of Ybor City, the Latin Quarter of Tampa. Nick didn't want to be a cigar worker like his father, but by the time he was seventeen, he had become fascinated with the union organizers who had come from the north to recruit members. He liked their style and swagger, and he didn't shy away from their sometimes-violent activities.

Violence always seems to engender more violence, and to attract those who are waiting in the shadows to feed off of the spoils—like jackals at a kill. Nick formed alliances and connections with people who were not really like him—people who had a great capacity for evil. Now that he was twenty-five and maturing, and coming under the influence of older members of his family who he respected, he was trying to lead a new life. But his old cronies seemed to be constantly around and totally oblivious to any desire of his to break ties with them. He admired people like Judge Jenkins, who had once helped him, and he was attracted to girls like Grace—girls from respectable families who were interesting and intelligent, but who still knew how to have a good time.

Nick was happy to see Grace again, and a little relieved that he hadn't scared her too badly at their previous meeting. He greeted her more calmly this time with his usual friendly manner.

"Hey, toots; I was a little worried after you left the other day. I didn't know you were coming with the judge, but I'm glad to see you. Judge, you look good with a blonde on your arm. You should get out more often."

"Nicky! Judge Jenkins isn't like you, you know," Grace answered huffily. "He's the nicest man in town, and he doesn't need a girl with him just to show off. This is serious business, anyway. I'm not in the mood to flirt today."

"Oh, that's alright, Grace," said the judge, as he held out her chair. "Let the young man have his fun. I'm upset about all of this, certainly, but when I was younger, I never missed a chance to flirt with a pretty girl. Life is too short, sugar. I know that better than anybody else. Let's just have a little something to eat, and then we can talk about this tragedy."

Lilly's father remained mostly quiet while the two young people talked and ate. It was good being with them, he thought. He hadn't been around his daughter very much in the last few months, and he still missed his wife.

Most of the people in the small cafe were leaving, and the judge felt it was time to get what knowledge he could from the young man. "Nick, I don't have to tell you that I've had plenty of experience in dealing with unsavory people, but the Moss family is something else altogether. Now, apparently, you know these people quite well and are somewhat in their confidence. Now don't misunderstand; I'm not suggesting that you're an interested party in this commerce of theirs. But my question is: What do you know about this, and what are they likely to do from here on?"

Nick put down his demitasse cup of thick, sweet *cafe solo*, wiped his mouth, and took a deep breath before he began. "Judge, Frank Moss is not somebody who you want any dealings with at all. That man has done a lot of harm to people—even people who you would think would be safe from him. It wouldn't matter if you were the damn governor; if you cross him, he'll come after you—or he'll have Ivan come after you. I don't know if you've seen his son since he quit boxing, but I swear to God, he's bigger than he was then."

Grace let out a worried sigh and shifted nervously in her chair. "Nicky, he's the one that's friendly with you. Can't you tell him to leave Lilly and her papa alone? They aren't responsible for anything Mac has done."

"Doesn't matter, toots. The Mosses won't let anybody steal from them; they'll get their money one way or the other. I don't think they've given up on finding Mac, though. The fact is, they would rather take it out on him. I guess the thing we need to know is this: Do you think Mac has their money, or at least, can he get it before too long?"

"Well, this is what we know, Nick," the judge answered. "We believe Mac is in New Orleans. Lilly received a letter, which he posted from there. He indicated to her that he had written a check to someone for around twenty-thousand dollars, but we know today that it won't be honored. The funds are no longer in place to cover it."

Nick tried hard to stifle an incredulous smile. "A check to the Moss family? I don't believe so, Judge. There may be some parts of their business that are straight up enough for bank records, but not this one. Besides, you've got a big problem there, Judge. Mac is into them for a lot more than that. Ivan Moss may be a criminal, but he's a straight talker. He told me that Mac owes him thirty-two thousand. If they don't get it all—well—what else can I say?"

"Tell Ivan where he is then, Nicky—just tell him where Mac is!" Grace was starting to get dizzy, and the gin from the night before was making her irritable.

Judge Jenkins patted her shoulder while smiling apologetically at Nick. "Now, calm down, sugar; we didn't come down here to give Mr. Cancello orders."

"That's alright, Judge; Grace is probably right. They always appreciate information. Maybe it'll keep them from bothering you and your daughter, at least for a little while. Let me ask you something, sir. Do you still have any—well, how can I say this—any feelings for your son-in-law?"

Lilly's father took a deep breath and looked away for a moment. "I don't think so, Nick," he said, shaking his head. "No, I don't. None at all."

Chapter 6

Lilly could hear every tick of every clock in the house. She had been waiting alone for her father to return, and now that she was feeling stronger, she wished she had gone with him. She also wished that everything, including Mac, would just go away. Maybe these people would find some other lives to invade or get interested in some new way to take other people's money. After all, they had certainly wormed their way into her life easily enough. Mac was supposed to be an intelligent man, but he had been ensnared as easily as a blind rabbit. Surely there were other men out there somewhere who the Moss family could now turn their attention to.

Her thoughts were suddenly interrupted by the opening of the front door and the voice of her best friend. "Feeling better there, kiddo? You look better, anyway. Doesn't she, Judge?"

"Let me feel your cheek, sugar. Why yes, I believe you're back to normal."

"Papa, tell me what was said. What did you find out?"

Lilly's father didn't answer right away, but instead turned to Grace. "Would you please give me leave to speak with Lilly alone for a while? It's not that I have anything to say that I don't want you to hear; and certainly you have been in our confidence in this matter, but I—"

"Oh, by all means, Judge; I'm going up to talk with Mama, anyway. Please, make yourself at home."

Lilly's father took his time to settle into the sofa next to his daughter, collecting his thoughts as he did so. "Sugar, I hope you never see that husband of yours again. How in the world someone of his background and supposed good character could form such connections is a mystery to me. But what is even more troubling, is his ability to obtain your apparent complicity in this enterprise."

The judge could see that his daughter's lip was beginning to tremble slightly, and he immediately softened. "Sugar, I don't mean to upset you. Sometimes, the old trial lawyer in me rears his head, even when I don't need him. But please, help me to understand how you came to this trouble, or perhaps I should say, how it came to you."

"Papa, I wish I knew. You know I'm not a weak person; you've always said I had Mama's temperament, and I've thought about that lately. I should have been able to think for myself. After all, women can vote now, for goodness sakes. It's a very strange thing, but when Mac looks you in the eye and tells you how things are going to be, it somehow makes sense. He went on and on to me about the sawmill closing. He said there was no future in anything like that anymore. He said the men in town knew all about which businesses would be booming after the war, and he had to get in with them."

"But, sugar, you cannot call what Mac was doing a proper or legitimate business. Surely you are aware of that."

"Of course I am, Papa, but somehow Mac convinced me that Frank Moss was just a businessman like any other. He kept telling me that the war had changed everything, and that people like Frank Moss had to do whatever they could to compete with the big companies up north—the ones who had made so much money with war contracts. According to Mac, Ivan was always talking about new businesses they would get into—airplanes and radios and such."

"Sugar, if you had only come to me sooner, I would have been able to help you see the dangerous path down which he was leading you. I don't want to condemn you, though, and you mustn't berate yourself for this. You are certainly not the first person who has been beguiled by a glib tongue."

"I'm sure that I am not, Papa, but my weakness hasn't hurt me only. I'm afraid of what I've done to you. Mama always talked about how well things worked out when we came here from Savannah—how quickly you were accepted in the legal circle, and in society in general. How will you be received now when it becomes known that your daughter is mixed up with Frank Moss?"

"Not very well, Lilly. That is a bit of ground on which we must tread very carefully. The people here are no different from those in Savannah; they are my friends now, but they will turn their backs in no time at all. Oh, they will be titillated by scandal, you can be sure, and it will fill their conversation for a few days, but, in the end, they will want none of it. That is why we must keep this quiet. It is bad enough that the Morgans know, but we need their help. I have no doubts as to their discretion, but no one else need find out."

Lilly's father got up from the sofa and stood silently in front of the window for a few moments. By the way he rubbed his fingers in his palm, Lilly could tell he was coming to a decision.

"Sugar, let's allow this thing to rest for the time being," he said. "I believe, from my conversation with Nick Cancello, that Frank Moss and his son will attempt to find Mac. I guess I should mention that I told Nick that Mac was in New Orleans. That information is certain to get to the Moss family. For now, I don't want to do anything else. Evan is due to come home next week. I think he has decided to work with me for a while before he makes a decision on his law studies. I believe he will have to be told about this because it would surely be difficult to keep it from him."

"What am I to do in the meantime, Papa? I'm afraid, but I can't just wait and do nothing."

"Well, first of all, I want you to stay here with Grace. Evan will be will staying with Aunt Maggie and me, and I don't know if she's up to more than that. But please stay away from the lake house, sugar, even if Grace is with you. It scares me to death to think you were out there alone for a week."

After her father left for his office, Lilly climbed the stairs to Grace's room. Grace was in her mother's bedroom down the hall, but came to Lilly as soon as she heard her come up. "Everything all right with you and your papa, honey?" she asked matter-of-factly.

Lilly sat on the edge of the bed and looked vacantly at the floor. "Yes, I suppose it is, Gracie, but I don't think everything's all right with me. I may be expecting."

"Expecting what? Lilly! No! No, you're not—you can't be!" Grace held Lilly's face with both hands and searched her eyes frantically for any clue that what she was hearing was false.

"I think I am, Grace. I'm late, almost five days now, and then I was sick this morning. You know I'm hardly ever sick like that."

"Oh honey, I'm sure it was just that stinky old gin from last night; I shouldn't have let you drink it. And you've been so upset lately. It's not that unusual to be late when your nerves are on edge. Wait a minute! How can you? You and Mac haven't—you know."

"Yes we have, Grace. I know. Don't look at me like that. It just happened—that's how he is. It was the first time in two months, but I couldn't hold him off forever."

"Well, you're not really sure yet, Lilly," said Grace, as she sat down on the bed beside her friend. "Are you going to say anything to your father?"

"You know, I almost did just now. He was so understanding about everything, that I thought I might as well just tell him, but now that I've had a moment to think about it, I don't think I will. The fact is, I don't know what I'm going to do. This is something I've tried to avoid for so long, and now it's happening at the worst possible time."

"But, honey, what else could you do but have it? You certainly wouldn't want your papa to find out that you stopped it. He would be horrified if he knew you did that. What if Mac comes back? What if all of this gets cleared up, and he straightens things out?"

Lilly stared at her friend for a moment, hoping that Grace didn't really believe the question she was asking. "Grace, I would never have said the things that I did about Mac if I were not dead serious. You know me better than anyone. Have I ever said things of that nature that I didn't mean?"

The truth of Lilly's question demanded silence, and neither of the women spoke for almost a minute. Lilly was thinking about Mac. She wondered if he was still acting as usual—calm and unruffled. Why was every trouble settled on her shoulders? If it weren't for her father and her best friend, she thought, she would run, too—as far as she could.

Chapter 7

Mac noticed the woman as soon as he entered the hotel lobby. Styles had changed drastically in the last few years, and women of means were keeping up with the times, each one trying to add her own flair or mark of distinction. But this was a woman who was trying too hard, a woman without the easy confidence of her wealthier sisters. Everything was a little off, not really audacious, but too dissonant to form a pleasing vision. She would certainly be pleasing in the right setting, Mac thought. She was as attractive as any woman he had seen in a long time. She had dark hair, like Lilly, but unusual green eyes. She was fleshier than his wife, and she moved in an open, unrestrained way. She was evidently free enough to be loitering in a hotel lobby, so it was apparent that she wasn't a working girl from one of the shops or offices. If she had money, or a man, she wasn't acting as though she did.

Whatever she was, she was just what Mac Harrison wanted. He wanted her because of the way he imagined she would feel next to him, and because he needed someone with him. Mac wasn't accustomed to going it alone. The best thing about her, he thought, was that she knew nothing about him; the troubles floating in his head were invisible to her. He could quit the desperate act he had been playing and just enjoy her company. And because of what she apparently was, he could use her to find Henry Wasson.

Mac picked up the newspaper lying on the arm of the sofa while the woman pretended to fix her makeup. He spoke while pretending to read. "Why are you trying to cover it up?"

"Cover what, sir?" she asked, not really surprised that she was being approached.

"Your face. Why are you trying to obliterate your face with powder? Don't you like it?"

"Of course I like it. Do you?"

"Like my face? Why shouldn't I?"

"No, cutie, *my* face. Do you like *my* face?"

"Cutie? Why, that's rather saucy. What happened to sir?"

"I didn't know you then; now I do."

"You know me? Gee, I'm sorry, but I don't remember being introduced to you, ma'am—or is it Miss?"

"Do you want to stand here all evening and play with words," she said, putting away her mirror, "or would you rather play with me? If you want to play with me, we'll have to go somewhere else."

Mac looked at her for the first time during this conversation and tried not to smile. It was time for a more serious discussion. "I take it that your presence is welcomed, or at least tolerated, in this hotel. I was just about to check in at the desk, and I want quiet enjoyment of my room. Is that going to be challenged if you accompany me?"

"Don't you think I have more sense than to waste my time in a place where I'm going to find trouble?"

Mac liked her direct manner. This was going to work out fine, he thought; things may come together in an easier way now—the way he was accustomed to. He registered at the desk, and ignoring the knowing glances of a few of the guests, walked confidently to the elevator, pushing the woman in ahead of him.

"Well, what's your name? I don't think you told me," he asked, in a gentler tone than he had used before, lifting up her chin with his finger.

"My name's Emily, if it's important to you. What's yours?"

"Uh—Evan—Evan Jenkins."

"Is it? You don't sound too sure about it."

"Listen, Emily; I'm not the kind of man who is accustomed to paying for a woman's company. I wasn't quite sure I wanted you to know my name, but yes, that's my name. No more questions for now—well, except for one. Can you stay for the night?"

"You seem to be a nice fellow. If that's true, I can stay as long as you want me to, but you have to promise to pay what I ask. I need the money. If I didn't, I wouldn't be doing this."

They went into the room in silence. There was no way in this hot, humid July night to make the occasion anything other than what it was. The slight, warm breeze coming through the open window only allowed them to sustain their breathing as they moved fitfully, drenched in each other's sweat in the coarse muslin sheets. For Mac, it was a release, and another form of escape from his enemies. For Emily, it was another night in her self-imposed purgatory.

Chapter 8

Emily Creighton's fall had been precipitous—a steep plunge from half a continent away. In a recent but forgotten past, she had moved through life to the music of old Baptist hymns. They were played by the minister's wife, her mother, in a grand white church in Kansas City. Now, all the music was different, and played to everyone's request but hers—at the whim of whoever was paying the band.

She was living on Rampart Street, in a rented bedroom above a dress shop. The troubles of her past were no more important than anyone else's around her; that was the reason she had decided to stay. Her sins did not scream out and beg for everyone's notice the way they had in Missouri. It seemed all the people here were living the same life: spending to catch up with the fast new age, and struggling to eat on whatever was left. There were plenty of ways to make money, but Emily had been taught only one.

She had learned long ago that almost everything about her was attractive to men. They all wanted to be with her. First it was young boys who pleaded for a simple touch or a kiss, and then the older ones, going off to war, who needed to become men in a single night. She almost never said no to any of them, and she was fascinated by the power she held. Everything she gave seemed to come back to her as nourishment to her spirit. Nothing else had ever done that—no matter what her parents had told her.

All of her thoughts and actions were supposed to be centered on Heaven; everything on earth was worthless and temporary. But she couldn't help wondering why these people at church were all so anxious to grow old and die. She felt alive. If God wanted only spirits in Heaven, why did He give her this body on earth?

Emily never found an answer. She found trouble and guilt and rejection. It would not have bothered her if these were people she cared little about, but the truth was, she loved them all. Her parents and grandparents and everyone else at the church were the best people on earth, she thought. They were good and kind, and they would have forgiven anything in time. But she couldn't bear the idea that she had failed them. She almost never thought about them now, though; Kansas City was a world away, and today, like most other days, she was waking up with a man she didn't know.

He was still sleeping, like so many of the others, with no apparent care and no place to be. Emily had been awake for a while, roused by the heat and the noise below. She was studying his face and trying to guess at his life. He was younger and more handsome than most. His body was lean and muscled, but his clothes and manner told her he wasn't a workman. He didn't look like a businessman either, she thought; they were usually pasty and fat. Politicians were easy to spot; they were loud and talkative, but this man was quiet. He wasn't unpleasant, she decided; if he wanted her to stay awhile, she probably would.

Emily slipped out of bed quietly and washed at the hand basin. When she returned, Mac was just waking up. "Well, Mr. Jenkins," she said; "are you coming around?"

"What? Oh—yes—I guess I am. I suppose you want something to eat."

"The way your dog or cat would, I imagine."

"No, I didn't mean that. Look, I'm sure you're hungry; I am. I'm not very sociable in the morning without coffee at least. Can you be seen in the hotel restaurant, or should we find some other place?"

Emily was slightly surprised at the invitation; it didn't happen often. "It would be best to go across the street," she answered, after a moment's thought. "It's a nice place, and we can sit in the back."

Mac washed up, and they left the room in the same unashamed way they had entered. At the cafe, they were both hungry and ate without speaking. Mac lingered over the remains of his coffee and silently pondered the proposal he was about to make.

"Emily, as I said last night, this is usually not the way I meet women. I noticed, though, that you seem to be a very straightforward lady, so I'll just say what I've been thinking. I'm going to be in New Orleans for a few more days. I would like you to stay with me. If I give you twenty dollars, will that be enough for the time being?"

It was an offer Emily had been hoping for. "It's enough, of course," she answered, "as long as there is nothing else that I need to know about. There are no other men—no other friends of yours or anything like that—I take it."

"Why on earth would you ask that?"

"Come now, Evan, if I can call you that; surely you're familiar with what girls like me are expected to do."

"I'm not expecting anything, Emily—nothing more than last night. I just need company, and maybe a little help with something.'

"Oh God! Don't tell me you're a policeman," she blurted out, loud enough for the other customers to hear. "If you are, I don't know how I missed it."

"I'm not a policeman. That's absurd. And please keep your voice down."

"Who are you then?"

"Look, it has nothing to do with who I am—nothing really. I'm a lawyer. I live in Tampa, Florida. My father has a law firm there. I have a friend who owes me some money—a gambling debt, I guess you could call it. My father doesn't approve of gambling, and he doesn't know I'm here. I'm supposed to be in Pensacola to see a client."

"Why would you come to a whore to help you find someone?"

Mac almost choked on his coffee. "Do you have to be so blunt? Can't you say it a different way?"

"It's what I am, Evan. If I couldn't say it, I wouldn't do it. I'm a whore, and I've always been one, even when I didn't make money at it."

Mac was uncomfortable with the direction of this conversation, but his curiosity was aroused. "I thought you said you wouldn't be doing this if you didn't need the money."

"I always make a sympathy plea when I ask for money." Emily felt she was somehow getting an advantage on this man, if only for a moment. "Are you so naive that you don't know when you're being hustled?" she asked, looking him straight in the eye.

For the second time in his life, Mac was dealing with a woman who didn't wilt at his command right away. This one may have more thorns than Lilly did in the beginning, he thought. However, he had little time to interview a line of applicants for the situation. She would have to do.

"He's someone who likes to spend money on women like you," Mac continued. "I thought you might know him. His name is Henry Wasson."

Emily appeared to be only half listening as she held up her mirror and looked at her freshly applied lipstick. "I may," she said, nonchalantly, "but I don't know that name. Men don't always give their real names to whores. You're a lawyer, Evan—surely you've had experience with people who lie."

Chapter 9

The real Evan Jenkins stepped off the train and into the arms of the sister who had not seen him since Christmas. Lilly's happiness at seeing her little brother made her realize that there was more to life—and more going on in the world—than her worries about Mac Harrison and his violent cronies. "Where have you been, you little stinker?" she said, as she hugged him tightly. "I thought you would be home after you graduated in June."

"You mean even a college degree doesn't free me of that name?"

"I'm still your older sister, and you're still a brat. I can call you whatever I want."

"So, who's the fancy blonde you brought with you?" Evan asked, winking at Grace.

Grace took her turn at hugging Evan and added a loud kiss on his lips. "You're gonna have to explain to me, too," she said smiling.

"Well, I've just been having a little fun with some of the guys from school. I guess Papa told you that I haven't quite decided on law school yet. I want to work with him a little bit first. I'm glad to be back home, though. Don't let anybody complain to you about Florida; summer is just as hot in Rhode Island. But it was nice there, and you know the Jenkins family has to keep up the tradition at Brown. So, what's new with you, Lilly? Where's Mac?"

"Mac's in New Orleans," said Grace, not allowing Lilly to answer and ignoring the elbow to her ribs. Your sister doesn't want to get into this right away, but your papa has already said you should know about it, so I don't see any point in dilly-dallying."

"Gracie, what's the rush?" said Lilly, getting between them. "I'm not going to air this out in front of everybody at Union Station. Anyway, the poor guy's had a long trip; let him catch his breath."

Evan had learned from long experience not to intervene when the two friends were hashing something out. He quickly changed the subject and put aside his curiosity while the three of them, and all of his luggage, squeezed into Aunt Maggie's Oldsmobile. As they drove away from the station, Lilly and Grace both tried to tell the story at once to an astonished Evan. Lilly's fears about her condition had been forgotten for the moment, however, and would remain a secret.

The three young people didn't notice a man standing at the corner of the building. Ivan Moss threw down his cigarette and kicked the red-brick wall of the depot. He had been standing there for what seemed like an hour, trying to find shade in the noonday sun and hoping that the passenger being picked up was Mac. He had visited the lake house that morning and found no one there. Driving back through town, Ivan passed Union Station just as Lilly and Grace were getting out of the car to go in. He was surprised to see the woman he had been looking for. He hoped that her reason for being at the depot would save him a trip to New Orleans, and more than that, save him from the increasing wrath of his father.

Frank Moss was expecting Ivan at the Tropic. The man was accustomed to getting everything he wanted—when he wanted. He was not accustomed to waiting, and he made no exceptions for the son who was dreading this meeting. Just as Frank was finishing his Milanese steak and deviled crabs, Ivan shuffled in, his face flushed with frustration and his collar soaked with sweat.

"I thought I was gonna catch the prick today, Pop. I saw his wife at the train station, but she wasn't after him—just her brother, looks like. Maybe he's in New Orleans like Nick says."

"Son, I've had enough of this shit," said the older man, throwing down his napkin in disgust. "See, this is what happens when you bring in people you don't know, especially guys like him. I'm havin' enough problems with these people in New York as it is. I don't need this jerk stealing from me on top of everything else, but I also don't have time to chase this son of a bitch all over the country. You find him, and you get the money he owes you, or you got two choices: you either get it from his wife or you take it out of *your* money."

"You mean you want *me* to cover it, Pop?"

"That's exactly what I mean, Ivan. If you're gonna run these little deals, you're gonna have to back 'em up."

"Pop, I ain't losin' money like that!"

"Well it looks to me like you already lost it, Mr. Bigshot. You get your ass to New Orleans. If you don't come back with anything, you get started on that pretty little bitch he's married to."

"Should we be worried about messin' with her, Pop?"

"Son, what kinda question is that? You don't worry about messin' with *anybody*—you mess with the goddamn Virgin Mary if I tell you to—you understand me?"

Ivan understood. His mind was already in New Orleans.

In another part of town, another father and son were meeting. Judge Jenkins never thought of himself as a sentimental man; he always tried to be practical and reserved. But since the death of Elizabeth, the presence of his children could tug at his heart. The first glimpse of Evan coming through the door of his office caused his eyes to moisten and his voice to break. "Hey, Son," he said. "It's good to see you again. You're certainly looking good. That time off must have been just what you needed. Are you hungry?"

"I surely am, Papa. That's the one thing I haven't been doing the best at. Breakfast on the train wasn't too bad, though."

"Well, sit down, Son. I had Aunt Maggie make up some roast beef sandwiches for us, and there's two bottles of dope in a pail of ice water there. Tell me how you've been doing."

"Gosh, Papa, you better tell me how you've been doing first. Lilly and Grace gave me the whole story already. What a thing to come home to!"

Evan's father was relieved that he was spared the ordeal of breaking the news. He had been mentally struggling with the best way to begin. Now, however, he was concerned about the worried look on his son's face. Evan's first visit home after beginning college had been at the time of his mother's death, and his homecoming now should have been a happy occasion.

As the young man settled into a chair next to his father's large mahogany desk, Judge Jenkins was struck by the change in his son's appearance and manner. Most of the signs and traits of boyhood—the awkward exuberance and flippant speech—had vanished. Evan carried his tall frame with more ease and grace, he noticed, and his expression suggested an active, thoughtful mind.

Evan's father leaned back in his leather chair and began slowly, trying to lay out his thoughts on the subject at hand, without adding to his son's apprehension. "First of all, I'm doing fine. One of the benefits of a career in law is that it opens your eyes to the potential for mischief that exists in the human race. I ceased long ago to be shocked by anything, and I've learned that people are capable of incredible greed. The joys of a good home and productive working life don't seem to be enough for some. It's apparent that Mr. Harrison isn't satisfied with having a lovely wife and comfortable circumstances. He's more impressed, evidently, with the lives led by gangsters and racketeers. Of course, I never expected to confront criminal activity in my own family, but I shouldn't be surprised; it's no different than Dr. Morgan having to treat Grace for an illness. We'll get through this thing, Son, but I'm going to need your help."

"Do you think we'll ever see Mac again?"

"The way that I feel about him now makes me hope that we don't. But that, of course, creates a new set of problems. First of all, there is the status of your sister, both practically and legally. If Mac doesn't return, we will have to wait for the required amount of time and then file the necessary petitions for dissolution. What is more of a worry to me, though, is the uncertainty of his actions. There is the prospect of his appearing without notice and causing harm to Lilly."

Evan stiffened, got up from his chair, and began pacing around the room. "Papa, this is almost too much to deal with. It's bad enough that we may have to protect her from these hoodlums, but at least we know who they are and where they are likely to be found. The idea of Mac showing up unannounced, at any time he chooses in the foreseeable future, is frightening. We will never know what his intentions are—or even his state of mind."

"I know, Son, but it's important for all of us to remain calm and clear headed. The fact that this happened now, when you are home and able to help, is a godsend. Perhaps Elizabeth is watching over us from up there."

"Well, that's why I came home, Papa: to help you here at the office."

"That was my original plan, Son, but I have a different idea now. I want to act on it immediately, before things get more complicated. I'm thinking of leaving the firm. I want to move back to the lake and set up a small practice there. The area around the train depot in Calusa is getting thickly settled, and that always creates work in real estate and probate law. I can live with Lilly and still continue to practice. I know that she and Grace are wonderful friends, but she can't stay with the Morgans indefinitely."

"What do you need me to do, then?" asked Evan, reaching in to the pail of ice water and handing his father the small, green bottle of cola.

"I need quite a bit of help, Son. The first thing you need to do is to move in to the lake house. It will be some time before I will be able to finish with my obligations here. During the day, you can help me by setting up an office in the east bedroom. It has a fireplace, so it will be comfortable in cold weather. You should have time to visit with some of the people in Calusa, especially the businesses there, and let them know that I will be available for consultations. I'm sure there are quite a few of them who will be happy about not having to drive into Tampa to see a lawyer."

"All of that seems fine, Papa," answered Evan, looking somewhat disappointed. "I suppose I will have to put aside my plan to learn a little law, though. I wouldn't think there would be enough in a practice like that to keep me busy."

This brought an amused smile to Judge Jenkins' face. He reached forward and put his hand on his son's shoulder. "There will be enough for a beginning," he said. "Don't fret about missing the excitement of a larger firm in town. People in the country can get into legal entanglements just as deeply as anyone else. I don't expect you to stay with me for long, though. If you take to it, as I believe you will, you'll need to get started with law school. There is no need to go back up north, Son; there are plenty of good law schools in the south. You should think about going to Gainesville."

For the first time since graduating from college, Evan felt useful. As he sat quietly with his father and finished the sandwiches his aunt had made for them, he had conflicting feelings. He was glad to be home with his family, and proud of the responsibility he was being given. But there were foreboding thoughts about his sister just below the surface New Orleans is a long way from here, he thought; if Mama *is* watching over us, maybe she'll keep the son of a bitch there.

Chapter 10

Mac was lying on the bed in his hotel room, smoking a cigarette and trying to picture Lilly's face. He wondered if he would ever see it again, but strangely, the prospect of that not happening did not greatly disturb him. He was more worried about survival—not minimal survival with food and a roof over his head, but survival in the style of living he had attained. These few days in the hotel had been gratifying to his desires and had proven that he could buy everything he wanted—as long as he had the money. He liked the idea of being able to buy women. It was so simple. There was no need to cater to their whims and fancies. In fact, he wouldn't need to know that they had any. If one got to be troublesome, he wouldn't even have to waste his breath to quiet her; he would simply send her away and procure another one. He was almost lost in thought, fantasizing about the possibilities of such a system, when the current holder of this tenuous office opened the door and walked into the room. Emily was wearing the new clothes that Mac had bought for her, including a blue, sequined hat with arching feathers that brushed her cheek as she walked. She sat down on the corner of the bed, somewhat breathless, and waited for the smoke ring her employer was blowing to rise above her head. "I think I may have found him," she said calmly.

"Wasson?"

"Yes. If your description is accurate, I think I have. A girl who works in the dress shop below my apartment grew up in the Quarter, and she seems to know almost everybody. She says there are two brothers who trade in narcotics, and—"

"That's him!" said Mac, sitting up and putting out his cigarette. "There was a brother, but they split up; he went to Baton Rouge. That's the thing about Henry: he's so goddamn hard to get along with. I never had any trouble, though, because I let him think he was getting his way all the time, and he's so stupid that he believes it. So it was a girl in a dress shop that led me to him. Why did I have this idea that I needed someone like you to find him? Where is he?"

"Well, I don't know where he is right now, but Carlene knows where he spends time at night. There's a little joint called Leila's on Chartres Street. You can find him there, but don't go on Friday. Carlene says they always raid it then—just for show. The regular clientele just mill around for a few minutes and go back in, but kids and out-of-towners get shaken down."

"Well, Emily, it looks like you're going to meet a new customer," said Mac, who was more pleased with himself than he had been in almost a month.

Emily turned her back so that Mac would not see the disappointment on her face. She really wasn't up for this kind of thing. In the last few months, she had found a way to make a living without going into places like that, and she was enjoying it. She was also enjoying this extended stay with Mac. It was a new experience for her, and even though she had no illusions, even about the immediate future, she wasn't ready for it to end. Her silence didn't go unnoticed.

"What's the matter, Emily? Are you getting lazy on me? That's the problem with women: as soon as they know where their next meal is coming from, they think they can quit working for it."

"Does Mrs. Jenkins still have to work for it?"

"There's no Mrs. Jenkins. I thought I told you that already. Anyway, what business is that of yours? I'm paying you for your time—and paying you damn well, as a matter of fact. If you don't want to do what I tell you, you can hit the road. Just leave those new clothes on the bed. They would look better on a blonde, anyway."

Emily turned around again and pretended to look out the window. "Tell me what you want me to do," she said, in a voice much weaker than he had heard from her before. Even as she said it, she was regretting it. She had survived pretty well, she thought, by not letting herself be pushed around, and she didn't know why she was giving in now.

"It's a simple thing to do, Emily. I want you to go to that place tonight and attach yourself to him. You surely know how to do that without me telling you. I want you to get him drunk and then bring him back here."

"Are you afraid of him when he's sober?" she asked, regaining some of her spirit again.

"I'm not afraid of anybody; I'm just not stupid. I learned a lot in the war, and the one thing I learned that's the most useful is that you always exploit your enemy's weaknesses. You don't make a frontal assault on an entrenched position unless you have overwhelming numbers. I also am not in the habit of causing commotions in public places."

"Your enemy? My God, Evan, I thought this was just a gambling debt you were trying to collect. I'm sure if he has it, he'll pay up."

"Whoa, Emily! You're getting into something that's none of your business again."

Although she couldn't imagine why, Emily started to shake a little, and she bit her lip to stop it. "If it's not my business, then why am I helping you?"

Before he answered, Mac lit another cigarette and reached in his pocket for his money clip. "I'm going to say this one more time, Emily. Even a whore should be smart enough to understand it. I'm paying you to do whatever I want—not to ask questions about it. You either shut up and do it, or you'll have to put your old clothes back on and find some other hotel room where you can stick your legs up in the air for money. Have you got that?"

Emily looked up and bit her lip again. "You were a much nicer man the other night."

"I'm as nice as the situation demands, Emily. Here's another five dollars. Get some sleep and then get ready for tonight."

After dark, Emily walked the six blocks to Leila's. With almost every step, she wondered at the reason for her desire to help this man. She needed the money, of course, but there were easier ways to make it. The most troubling thing, she thought, was his changing manner.

He had been sweet and playful in the beginning, but now she was seeing a different side. At first she had written it off as frustration with his supposed troubles, but there was a disturbing hardness in his speech. She wondered at the real nature of the heart behind it.

Before Emily could change her mind, she found herself at the door of the establishment where she would reluctantly hunt her prey. The cafe had a marginally good business during the day, but it was now doing much better as a speakeasy at night. It got no more trouble from the police than any other place with a similar clientele.

After she entered the largely empty front section of the cafe, Emily followed piano music to a smoky back room already filled with people. They were mostly men, and fairly well dressed. She didn't know the few women there and was uncertain if any were her sisters in the trade. Prohibition had changed everything. All kinds of people were now going to such places as this to discreetly break the law—to clandestinely engage in an activity they had openly enjoyed just a short while ago. It made people act, and even dress, differently. Sometimes, it was difficult to know whether a particular person was a gangster or a librarian.

It took her a few minutes, but she finally spotted the man she believed was Wasson. He had thick, curly hair and a prominent nose, the way Mac had described. The thing that made her fairly certain was his rather big feet and cocky stance.

After ordering a cola (which automatically contained rum) she took a few sips to embolden her disposition and made her move toward him. "Henry! I thought that was you standing there," she said in a giggling voice, draping one arm over his shoulder. "Haven't seen you in a while."

Wasson looked at the woman with a confused but interested stare. "I've been around—here and there—you know. Who are you?"

"Oh come on, Henry. Were you that drunk when we got together? I know there were a lot of other girls there, but we had so much fun, I thought you would remember me."

"We got together?"

"We got together and together and together—for a long time, I remember."

Henry Wasson was still a little confused, but more than a little interested. "Well, maybe if we try it again, I won't forget this time. What was your name again?"

"Now, Henry, I'm insulted; I remembered yours. I'll give you the rest of the night to try to remember mine."

"Are we spending the rest of the night together?"

"Well, I hope so, silly. Why do you think I came over here to talk to you? But you're not in a hurry, are you? I've only had one little drink."

Emily had three more drinks before making a firm determination to stop. She was at her limit and knew she needed a reasonably clear head. Henry Wasson was under no such restriction and followed his normal course of drinking himself into euphoria, and even somewhat beyond that, into an agreeable delusion.

They walked clumsily and loudly to the hotel. Henry's confusion even extended to the fact of his not knowing whether this occasion would require payment for services or not. Either way, it didn't really matter to him; he had been living a reckless, carefree life for the past month, and this was just another new adventure.

Emily kept her arm around her catch as she fumbled for the key. Henry began lifting her blouse as they walked into the darkened room. In a swift and uncannily silent movement, Mac Harrison seized the startled man from behind, threw him onto the bed, and pinioned him with the full weight of his body. Emily gasped and retreated into the corner. She had led an adventurous life in the past year, but she had somehow avoided violence. She was unnerved by its ferocity. Henry let out an unmanly wail that was throttled by the hand at his throat.

The terror in Wasson's eyes was gradually replaced by a bewildered look of recognition. He choked out his words as the grip on his neck was loosened. "Jesus Christ, Mac! You tryin' to kill me?"

"Why shouldn't I kill you, you little creep? You just better be glad it's me and not Ivan Moss on top of you. Where's my money?"

Henry Wasson smiled and then began to laugh in an amused but almost maniacal way. His speech was slurred but unusually coherent. "There ain't any money, Captain. There hasn't been for a long time. Everybody has been movin' in on me here—not small-time people like us—guys with all kinds of connections. I had to pay them all off. Jimmy was smart to go to Baton Rouge; I shoulda gone with him. But hell, I'm tired of all this business—I just wanna enjoy life. Why don't you do the same? Just move somewhere else. Frank Moss don't care about little fish like us. He'll get on to somebody else in no time."

Mac was dazed by Wasson's revelation. He only momentarily thought about reestablishing his grip at the man's neck. There was little use, he thought; it would just be one more thing to worry about. He got up from the bed and pulled his captive up by the collar. He motioned for Emily to open the door and then kicked Henry through it before closing it behind him.

"Evan, why did he call you Mac? And what's all the other stuff about?" asked Emily, still shaking, and now fully sober. "You told me he may be involved in narcotics, but it doesn't sound like something a lawyer would be mixed up in."

Mac's mind was still whirling. He answered almost automatically, with no real conviction, and without his previous disdain for her curiosity. "He calls everybody Mac; it's a common nickname. He owed me money; that's all there is to it. I don't know what else he was talking about. Listen, I've got to get some sleep." Mac rubbed his head as though he had a headache. "Here's five more bucks; why don't you go back to your place for the night."

Emily took the money and walked out in silence, regretting her role in the attack on that strange little man, and vowing to never again be an accomplice to vengeance. After she left, Mac spent several hours trying to reorient his thinking. Tomorrow, he would cash the check. He wasn't sure why, but he thought about taking Emily with him. He couldn't think of a good reason not to.

Chapter 11

Mac Harrison always slept on his left side, on the edge of the bed. When he woke on the morning after his assault of Henry Wasson, he was staring at a blank wall. He stared for a full twenty minutes, trying to picture what his life would now become. No vision emerged from the flat, white space.

There would be the money, he hoped, from the check, but he could see nothing beyond that hollow fact. He had been accustomed to making plans, to devising strategies, and he enjoyed pulling the strings of whatever persons he found useful, like a determined and skillful puppeteer. Now, he imagined a dull and empty life. He was young, but there was something in his mind that told him it would be hard to start over again. The practical quality of Mac's nature began taking hold, however, and he started to think about the things he had to do. One of those things was to make a decision about Emily. As much as he tried to convince himself that there were thousands more just like her, there was still something in her, he thought, that was appealing. He wasn't quite sure if he was finished with her yet or not.

He had to leave New Orleans, though, and head to his friend's bank in Birmingham. He would have to drive down Rampart Street and past Emily's apartment above the dress shop. He could stop and ask her to go with him. If she didn't want to go, his decision would be made for him. He was in too dreary a mood to really care, anyway.

An hour later, Mac was standing on the sidewalk outside the hotel. He placed one foot on his suitcase and smoked a cigarette while the porter brought his car around. The sight of his shiny, new Packard made him feel a little better. Without waiting for the car to stop, he tossed his luggage through the open rear window and pushed his way past the perplexed hotel servant, who meekly accepted the dime pressed into his hand.

Mac drove up Canal Street and turned down Rampart. As he glanced in the mirror, he was struck by his own cold, dispassionate expression. The sight deadened his feelings even more. As the traffic thinned, it just seemed easier to keep going—to leave New Orleans and Emily behind—to get his money and get on with whatever was left of his life. He pressed the accelerator down harder and tried to keep his mind empty of thought. Soon, he was crossing the causeways over the marshy bayous outside of town and shielding his eyes against the Louisiana sun.

The long drive through Alabama gave Mac time to lay out a plan. As he followed the bumpy roads through thick woodlands and small towns, the former captain tried to apply his military experience to the matter at hand. By the time he passed through the high stone bluffs surrounding

Birmingham, he had decided on a course. Because his visit to the bank would eventually be revealed to people in Tampa, he would need to do something to divert the attention of anyone following him.

A feinting move to the east would be a good beginning, he decided. He could leave a trail of evidence half way up the east coast and then head toward the west—as far as he could go. California would be good, he thought, or even Seattle or Alaska—far away from Ivan Moss and anybody else who would want to harm him. Lilly would probably not be one of those, but he certainly did not want to endure her censure, and even worse, the pious disdain of her family.

Mac stopped at the best hotel in the center of Birmingham just long enough to bathe and change clothes. There were plenty of cheaper places nearby, but he wanted to maintain the high standard he had set for himself. He was calling on a brother officer, he reasoned; it wouldn't do to mix with the common crowd. He found the building where Major William Selwyn was resuming his civilian occupation as a bank president. His former superior greeted him warmly and was obviously surprised and happy to see him. "My goodness, Captain Harrison, I hardly recognized you in that suit of clothing," he said, his hand extended across his desk. He thought briefly about coming around the desk to hug his old friend, but something in Mac's demeanor made him change his mind. "You always did cut quite a figure, though," he continued, "and I must say that you still do. The last time I saw you, you were heading to Florida. What brings you up here?"

"Just passing through, Major. I'm on business and I need the services of a good bank. I knew you had always planned to come back here after the war, so I naturally thought about seeking you out. I wanted to see you again, anyway, and I thought I could take care of my business at the same time."

"Well certainly; I'm glad you thought of me. First of all, Mac, let's drop these army titles. I never was much of a soldier, anyway—at least not as good a one as you. But tell me, what are you doing with yourself these days, and what can the bank help you with?"

"I'm in the lumber business in Tampa. You know, it's really been a wonderful change after the army, but it surely has some difficult aspects. I was on my way to Pittsburgh to purchase a new boiler for the sawmill. Everything seemed to be in order at first, but then, I got a telegram from my partner saying that the foundry had changed the payment arrangement. They want cash, and I left town with only a check, of course. I was wondering if you could accept my personal check for cash, and then I could be on my way. We need the new boiler desperately."

"Uh—sure, Mac. I don't see why not. What's the amount?"

"Twenty thousand," said Mac, shifting in his chair and trying to wipe the sweat from his upper lip.

"Twenty thousand! That's an awfully large check, and it certainly must be an awfully large boiler. My brother had a sawmill up here for years, and I know he never paid that kind of money for machinery. Are you sure about this, Mac?"

"Things have changed, Major—uh—Bill, I mean. We have to keep the sawmill up to modern standards."

"Well, I need to look into our cash supply, Mac. Let me have the check, and I'll see what I can do. Make yourself comfortable; this may take a little while."

As William Selwyn walked out of the office, Mac couldn't see the serious and somewhat wary expression on his face. The banker walked past his secretary and down to one of the clerks on the main floor. He spoke with the same voice and expression he would have used if he had been changing a child's paper bill for a silver dollar. "Mr. Preston, I need you to make a quick telephone call for me to the Peninsula Bank in Tampa, Florida. I'll be right over here with Mr. Walters. Just wave to me when you have them on the line."

On his way to the head teller's station, Mr. Selwyn stopped at the large mullioned window overlooking the street and gazed at the tall, green sweet gum trees lining the park. The sight took him back to Europe, to the war, and to all of the men whose lives were so closely entwined with his. He had counted on men like Captain Harrison for his very survival. They had all done heroic things and had seen horrible images of death and destruction in that awful trench warfare. It had all ended so suddenly. They said their goodbyes and then, in what seemed like an instant, were transported back to their former lives.

This unexpected reunion with Mac had begun with high emotions, but now it seemed almost barren of meaning. His former comrade was coming to him on the occasion of a mundane business errand. There was something wrong, he thought, with every aspect of it. First of all, Mac's expression and demeanor were different than what he remembered. The young soldier had always been earnest and straightforward in his manner, but now, even though his story seemed plausible, he appeared cagey and insincere.

These thoughts were interrupted by the clerk's officious speech. "Mr. Selwyn, I have the Peninsula Bank on the line for you."

"Thank you, Mr. Preston. Hello, this is William Selwyn at Southern Commerce Bank in Birmingham. Who am I speaking to, please?"

"My name is Raymond Lassiter, sir. What can we do for you today?"

"Thank you for taking my call, sir. Just a brief inquiry is all. This involves a fairly large transaction. It's for an old friend, but I have a board of directors to answer to, just as you have. The amount drawn on your bank is twenty-thousand dollars. He's your customer, and I'm sure you know him well: Captain—excuse me—Mr. McKinley Harrison "

After a silence of nearly fifteen seconds, Raymond Lassiter haltingly answered. "That—uh—that check is not going to be any good, Mr. Selwyn. I'm sorry; did you say Mr. Harrison is an old friend of yours?"

The Birmingham banker was somehow not as surprised as he ordinarily would have been, and under any other circumstances, he would want to know more. But there was a sudden tightening in his throat and a hollow feeling in his stomach. He just wanted to end the conversation.

"Yes, sir, we served together in Europe," he said weakly.

"Well, there are people here, sir, his wife in particular—"

"Mr. Lassiter, I'm sorry. I have something pressing, but thank you—thank you—I appreciate your time. Good day to you, sir."

The former major sat quietly for a few moments after hanging up the telephone. He then walked slowly up the stairs to his office, the check hanging limply from his hand. His legs got heavier and his mouth drier with each step. He walked into the room in silence and sat down slowly at his desk, wetting his lips and clearing his throat for what he had to say. "Mac, I'd love to be able to help you, but it seems there's some impediment to the cashing of this check. I don't know the nature of it; I didn't inquire. I'm sorry. I wish you luck, of course. Again, I'm sorry."

Mac heard few of these words. A loud rushing noise in his ears had begun as soon as he saw the check dangling uselessly from Bill Selwyn's hand. His own futile words sounded wooden and meaningless, and seemed to come from far away. What appeared to be a plausible plan, now felt ridiculous and childish. His deceits had never caused him humiliation before, and he didn't know how to act. He struggled to his feet and clumsily attempted a handshake before stumbling through the door and down the stairs.

Mac walked out of the bank and down the sidewalk toward his car, insensibly bumping into almost everyone he passed. He climbed behind the wheel of the Packard and pulled away from the curb and into traffic. His driving was jerky and reckless as he headed through town toward the highway. For a few miles, he made a half-hearted attempt to drive east as he had planned, but it suddenly seemed as ridiculous as everything else he had recently done. He pulled to the side of the road and sat with his hands in his lap, numbly staring into the distance.

Chapter 12

Dr. Morgan took off his lab coat and washed his hands while his nurse was helping Lilly dress in the next room. He then sat down at his desk to write a few notes and gather his thoughts.

Thomas Morgan was a quiet, gentle man who loved his medical practice and his family. His daughter was his only child and she was a joy to him. He had hoped to see her married—if that would make her happy. But Grace was a lively spirit who would follow her own wishes. Her exuberance was contagious, and almost nothing ever saddened her. Dr. Morgan wondered how well she was coping with the new view of the world that she was now seeing through her best friend's troubles.

Judge Jenkins had explained it all to him. It in no way changed his opinion of Lilly. He had taken to her as quickly as his daughter had, and he was sure that his first impression was still valid. His opinion of Mac was also unchanged. Thomas Morgan always thought he could spot a liar, and it had been a difficult burden to conceal his feelings.

Now, just as that burden was lifted, he was being asked to shoulder another. Lilly sat across from his desk and pleaded her case. 'Dr. Morgan, I just can't tell Papa, yet. I don't know how; everything is wrong. What am I supposed to say—that everything will be wonderful— that we'll all be able to live together in Mama's old house at the lake? I don't even know what's going to happen to us. Frank and Ivar Moss want their money. It's more than I have."

Dr. Morgan leaned forward on his desk and looked sympathetically into Lilly's face. "Your father will take care of you and the child, I'm sure," he said softly. "I'm also sure that he'll take care of these people. He's a lawyer, Lilly, and people tell me he was a wonderful judge. He knows the law, and he knows how to deal with these things."

"These people don't care about the law, Dr. Morgan. If they did, they would be in some legitimate business. They do whatever they want, and they get whatever they want. There are a lot of things you can say about my husband, but he isn't a coward. I know what he did in the war. If he's running from the Moss family, there's a reason, and I don't think I have to tell you what that is."

Grace's father sighed deeply and leaned back in his chair. He tried to draw on the things he had learned in life: the moral lessons of his Methodist upbringing and the practical observations of his scientific training. Christianity, as his mother had explained it, was based on kindness and forgiveness. But turning the other cheek to vicious criminals seemed ridiculous. His thoughts on medicine, on the other hand, were simple and empiric: some conditions were always fatal; others were not. Patients were either getting better or getting worse; almost nothing was ever static and unchanging. Dr. Morgan was ever the optimist, even in the face of disturbing odds, and saw no good purpose in predicting the worst.

He suddenly realized that there was a more important matter at hand. The failures and fears of the young woman in front of him, as grave as they may be, were unknown to the life now beginning in her womb. The physician wanted to somehow capture Lilly's mind and direct her thoughts away from the past, away from the ominous signs of the present, and toward a not-too-distant horizon that may not be as bleak as she imagined.

He began slowly and haltingly, and his eyes, which usually always focused on the recipient of his thoughts, occasionally wandered in search of his words. "Lilly, I know that young people don't always like to hear about the wisdom that comes with age. And I know you believe—and I believe also—that you are an intelligent and capable woman. But there are some things in life that you can only learn by experience. I've learned that events and circumstances have a wide array of outcomes. Situations in which all of our best efforts fail, sometimes have endings as desirable as those in which we succeed at every turn."

"Dr. Morgan, I'm not sure that I even know what a desirable outcome would be," Lilly answered. "I've been pretending to be happy. I've led everyone to believe that I loved my husband and that my life was unfolding in the way I had planned. I was supposed to be taking my place in the family and giving my father and brother something to be happy about—something they lost when Mama died."

"Lilly, your father and Evan love you more than you can imagine," said Dr. Morgan as he took the young woman's hand. "Not for what you do, but for who you are. I can say the same thing for Grace—and you can, too. The two of you couldn't be closer. Do your feelings for her depend on whatever life she has set for herself?"

Lilly wrapped her arms around her waist and trembled slightly as tears welled up in her eyes and spilled down her cheeks. "No," she answered and wiped the tears with the back of her hand.

"Perhaps you should consider going away for a time, Lilly. You can't live in fear, and you have important things to think about. The demands of this situation with Mac would be better met by your father. He has Evan to help him now. You've carried this for too long as it is. Is there anyone in Savannah you can stay with?"

"Papa's oldest sister, Aunt Eunice, still lives there. I'm worried about Papa, though."

"You've worried enough, Lilly. I certainly won't do anything else to trouble you. I won't say anything about your condition. Mrs. Morgan doesn't know, and I don't have any reason to tell her. Keep it between you and Grace if you wish, but don't do anything you'll be sorry for. Just take care of yourself, Lilly. Try to find a reason to be happy again."

Chapter 13

"It's so marshy around Savannah," said Lilly, as Grace pulled armloads of clothes from her closet. "It makes no sense for us to take the car. We'll just get stranded somewhere, and then Evan will have to dig us out of the muck. Evan's got his hands full trying to help Papa, anyway, and he's just getting settled here. The poor thing hasn't had a real home for four years now. The train will be fine."

Grace couldn't argue. As much as she liked to be in control of her movements, Lilly's wishes had to come first. Grace was just happy to be going away with her, anyway. She had never seen Savannah, and she was getting bored with her life in Tampa. And maybe she would get her best friend back again, she thought. For the past year, she had watched her slip further away. Every time she saw Lilly, she could see in her eyes, and in her manner, the signs of a new battle, new wounds inflicted by the soldier husband who was fighting a mercenary war.

"How do they dress in Savannah?" said Grace, holding up one of her flapper dresses and trying to get Lilly to smile. "Will I be arrested in this?"

"Only if you're carrying a flask, and even then, it depends on the company. People are not that different there. My cousin Cassie sent me some photographs of a wedding. It was at one of the nicer hotels in town. Everyone was drinking, and Papa said a lot of the people in the picture were politicians. I've even heard that President Harding drinks in the White House, so why shouldn't everybody else?"

"You shouldn't be drinking, though, honey," said Grace, almost to herself. "Not for a while, anyway."

Lilly put down the blouse she was folding and looked at Grace. She put on the same slight smile they both always used when messages were received in this fashion—messages weighted with hope and delivered to make an appeal. She kept up her stare until Grace was forced to retreat.

"What? Come on, honey—you know what I mean."

"You really want me to have this baby, don't you?"

"Of course I do, Lilly. And I think you do, too. Look, I know we agreed to not talk about it. Papa even told me to leave you alone for a while. I won't say anything else; let's just finish packing and get on our way. We have a lot of other things to talk about, anyway, and the train will be fun. But I still think you shouldn't drink anymore."

"Grace!"

"O.K. I'm sorry. Let's just get ready."

Evan took them to Union Station the next morning. While they waited to board, they talked to Evan about his new mission in life. "How much have you done out there?" asked Lilly. "Isn't it hard setting all that up by yourself?"

"Oh, I have help. Mr. Nichols from the sawmill has been helping me make the bookcases. They're almost finished. That's why I'm in town today. Papa has about half of his books ready to move, and I'm going to take them out there this afternoon."

"Has Mr. Nichols said anything about Mac," asked Lilly, who looked somewhat uneasy about the closeness of her husband to this subject.

"Oh, he's said a lot, but I didn't think you would want to hear any of it."

"It depends on what he said, Evan. Is it anything I would be upset about? If it is, I probably don't want to know about it. If it's anything that would be helpful, that's a different thing."

"He's just been worried about you, Lilly; they all have down there. Mac hasn't been easy to work for. Everything that's gone wrong with him has been taken out on the men. He was away from his job so many times, and they're not stupid; they knew he was up to no good. They've all known you for a long time, though. Some of them have worked there since we were kids, and they all like Papa. Mr. Nichols said he would keep an eye out for Mac. If he shows up, or if he even hears that he may be headed back here, he'll let me know."

"You know, Evan, I sometimes get the feeling that Mac will just show up and act as though nothing has happened. That's the way he has been through all of this. He's always denied that he has done anything wrong, and he expects me to believe that everything he does is for the purpose of making me happy. But it's not true. That episode with the necklace is a good example. Everybody knows that I've never been taken with such things. That was just something to make him feel superior. In his mind, having his wife wear something like that elevated him above all the other people around here. I've always given gifts to see the joy in someone's eyes. But to Mac, everyone's eyes are just mirrors for his vanity. Mac doesn't even look for admiration, only envy, and that is something you can always buy if you have enough money."

"Maybe that is the best reason for his not coming back," said Evan, whose quiet, thoughtful way of speaking had greatly impressed his older sister. She had noticed the changes in his manner, just like her father had, and now she was sorry to be going away from him. "Mac probably doesn't have any more money," Evan continued. "You told me he had gone through all of the cash at the house. What is left for him here? He may be afraid of Frank and Ivan Moss, but he's probably just as afraid of everybody's contempt."

Grace had been quietly listening. She had abandoned her usual talkativeness to allow Lilly to visit with her brother, but this was a subject she had strong feelings about. "Pity, I believe," she said.

"What did you say, Gracie?"

"Pity. He's more afraid of pity than anything else. That would be the true thing, wouldn't it? I mean, he could always dispute everyone's contempt. He's always right about everything—or he thinks he is. But he wouldn't be able to hide from their pity. I think that's what he's hiding from now. Mac has faced gunfire before; that's the worst thing the crooks can do to him. Pity would kill him just as easily, though, and probably a lot more painfully. Well, he doesn't have to worry about me, at least. He won't get anything from me except a crack on top of the head. I'll leave the pity to everybody else."

Grace could always make Lilly laugh. It was her constant gift, her constant act of kindness. She always knew when to use it, and in what doses. It didn't always work on fear, though—that was a much tougher thing. Fear required a gentle squeeze of the hand, a knowing look, or perhaps just silent understanding. Grace was ready with these, but more than anything now, she wanted to enjoy her best friend's company—enjoy the times they had together the way they had always done. So when the boarding call was made by the conductor, the energetic blonde pulled Lilly up by the hand and acted as excited as if they were going on a normal holiday trip.

Grace's sense of happiness was infectious. The two friends hugged and kissed Evan and hurried up the steps of the train car. Nothing in their voices or expressions suggested a flight from trouble or the beginning of a brooding exile.

Chapter 14

The sounds and smells were familiar. The fading voices of children playing in the twilight and the ancient scents of the old city stirred visions of her early childhood. But the sights—the houses, churches, and shops of Savannah—seemed different to Lilly. Everything looked smaller. The streets were darker and drearier than she had remembered. She wondered if the impression was true, or only a distorted reflection of her mood. She could recall no faces from the old square just off Bull Street, only that of her aunt.

Lilly sat alone in the front parlor and tried to remember why she had come here. She listened to her aunt talking to Grace in the next room. She imagined her friend listening politely at her aunt's dissertation, accompanied by photographs, on the Jenkins family history. It was mostly about the war, of course. Not the recent world war, but the important one, the one that had nearly exterminated the young men of Georgia. Lilly had heard the stories before. They had terrified her as a young girl, and they were still disturbing. They were about men trudging into a barrage of bullets as though it were blowing rain. They were about canon balls, which screamed murderously through the air, decapitating fathers and sons.

What would these people think of me? Lilly thought— not only the ghosts of her ancestors, but some of these men who were still alive—men who could never erase the fear and horror from their memory. Her own fears seemed small and cowardly, and the circumstances were sordid and devoid of any honorable justification.

After a while, the limits of Grace's interest and her ability to be social after a long, tiring train trip were tested. This fact was not lost on her indulgent hostess who excused herself to duties in the kitchen and suggested that the young woman look after her friend in the parlor. Grace no sooner walked into the room than she was met by Lilly's urgent question. It was delivered as though it had been held in deliberation and was now being released as a sudden understanding. "It wasn't really because of fear, was it, Gracie?"

"What, honey? What are you talking about?"

"We didn't come here because I was afraid, did we? I would feel so foolish if that was the reason. I hadn't even thought about it before your papa told me it would be the best thing to do."

"Well, I don't know about you, Lilly, but I was afraid for you. I've been worried about you for months, and then, when this latest thing happened, I was sorry that I hadn't done more to protect you."

"I know, Gracie. I've always known you would do anything for me, but I don't want to be afraid. I've never been like that. I hope I'm like Mama; she wasn't afraid of anything. She always had the idea that she was smarter and stronger than everybody else, man or woman. I've had a little time to think, and the distance has helped. I believe the reason for being here is to sort my life out and make the right decisions, to figure out what I need to do."

"About the baby?" asked Grace, in an almost apologetic voice, not quite sure if was a subject to be opened again.

"That's part of it, the biggest part, I guess. I'm trying to get a picture of the kind of person I'm going to be, the kind of life I'm going to have. It's all different now. I've thought about being alone, of course. I've thought about it a lot in the last year, maybe even longer than that. The thing is, Grace, I never imagined having a child with Mac, at least not after we had been together for a while and I began to see what he was really like. I tried to be so careful. I avoided him as much as I could, and when I couldn't, I tried everything I knew that would keep this from happening."

"Honey, why didn't you ever tell me you were going through that?"

"I don't know, Grace; it didn't seem right, I suppose. I was ashamed for feeling that way. I tried to imagine Mama doing such a thing, and I couldn't."

"Lilly, your mama wasn't married to Mac Harrison. She was married to the nicest, sweetest man anybody knows. I'm sure she would have had more children if she hadn't been sick. You had a reason for not wanting any, and I guess you have an even better reason now. But, honey, there's a difference now—you're already expecting. Isn't it too late?"

Lilly closed her eyes and remained silent for a moment. She then looked off into the distance and searched for the right words. "I don't know if it's too late. I'm going to find out, though. I'm going to find out a lot of things, and I'm going to decide about it while I'm here at Aunt Eunice's."

"Oh, honey, are you sure you want to do that?"

"Yes, Gracie, I am. I'm not sure about what I will finally do, but I'm sure that I will make a decision—one way or the other."

Lilly awoke to other familiar sounds and smells the next morning. A gentle easterly breeze was coming off the Atlantic, and as it blew along the Savannah River and rustled through the dogwood and camellias outside the window, it picked up the aroma of Low Country food being cooked in Aunt Eunice's kitchen. The sounds, which were barely audible above the wind, were the voices of the black servants speaking in Gullah, the beautiful language of the coastal Georgia and South Carolina slaves. It was more than a simple mixture of African and English words; it was a living heirloom—a record of contact between people of widely different origins who had been brought together by the institution of slavery. The distinctive pronunciations of mariners and overseers could still be heard, but above all was the verbal adroitness prized in the rice cultures of West Africa. The children and grandchildren of slaves still spoke it, even in the households of their white employers. It was something they could have for themselves during the days they spent in other people's homes. Lilly's aunt never tried to discourage it. She had learned a lot of it, herself, from her black nanny, like so many other white children of her class.

Lilly had forgotten much of it. She knew the phrases that her father still used when he was homesick for Georgia. The speech she heard now, while she was lying awake, impressed her with its lilting, musical quality, and she recognized the speaker as Bessie Mae, her parent's old cook who had been taken in by her aunt after the move. Lilly got dressed quietly and went down to the kitchen, happy that she would have some time before Grace and Aunt Eunice got up. Bessie Mae recognized her at once and modified her Gullah for Lilly's ears. *"Chil', is dat you? Lawd a mussy come lemme tek a look. Dey tell me you was comin' to Sawannuh. You jis' tun out pooty same lukkuh flower."*

Lilly hugged Bessie Mae and sat down at the kitchen table beside her. "I remember you," Lilly said, smiling and holding the woman's hand. "It seems so long ago, but Papa talks about you a lot. He really missed your cooking after we came to Florida. Where is your daughter? What was her name—Bernice?"

"Yaas'am, das fuh true. 'E 'bout you same age. 'E wu'kin' at de 'Piskubble chu'ch 'puntop Abercorn. I s'pose you don' haffuh wuk. I see lotta white oomen wu'kin' now, but you aunt say you hab a husban'. Bernice jump de broom, but she wuk same lukkuh mule."

"I did have a husband, Bessie Mae. I don't know where he is, but even if he comes back, he won't be coming in my house again."

"Oh, chil', dat ent a good t'ing. Why a man run off an lef' a nice wife like you fuh?"

"It's a long story, Bessie; I don't think you want to hear it."

"Well, das why you come up yuh all by you' own se'f. You jis' haffuh pray de lawd ketch you 'nurruh man, chil'."

Lilly smiled at this last remark. It was the furthest thing from her mind now. "Bessie Mae, if I tell you something, can I trust you to keep it a secret? I also want to ask you something—and that has to be an even bigger secret."

The woman put down the bowl she was holding and looked at Lilly with a serious expression that was a little bit unnerving. *"Yaas'am. Go on."*

"Well, let me jus: ask you a question. What can a woman—who is expecting a child—do if she doesn't want—if she can't really have—a child? Where can she go?"

Bessie Mae's expression was even more grave now, and she stared at Lilly for such a long time that Lilly was almost forced to withdraw the question. "Bessie, I—"

"I yeddy, chil'. You da try fuh pick me mout'. But you ax'me what a white ooman do. Das a diffunt t'ing an what a colluh ooman might do. You say weh 'e go? 'E ent go noweh. Colluh ooman hardly hab a nice place fuh hab a chil', but 'e still wantuh hab it—eb'ry chil' is a gif frum da lawd. But I 's'pec a buckruh ooman look to 'ese'f. Somebody tek care of it—somebody keep it hush an mek b'leew dey is tekin' out a 'pendix or sump'n'—t'row it in de trash like a rotten 'pendix. Wuffuh you wantuh t'ink 'bout dat? You ent haffuh worry 'bout 'nurruh mout' tuh feed. You get you bittle an clode frum you papa anyways. Ent dat fuh true?"

Lilly couldn't answer. She felt a little ashamed. When she first sat down with Bessie Mae, she felt a kinship. It was as though she were seeing a long lost member of her family. But the differences between them, she now realized, were stunning. Their experiences and expectations were created in different worlds. Whatever happened in her life, no matter how threatening, there would be someone there to protect her and to heal any injuries. The women in Bessie Mae's world, however, would face most crises alone, or at best, with commiserating friends and loved ones who were in no better position to provide help. But there seemed to be a will to survive, to create a new generation who would have it better.

It had been fifty-five years since the end of slavery, but Lilly knew that Bessie Mae's people had not come very far. She had heard the stories and read the old letters about the destruction of black families when slaves were sold. The freed slaves and their children had earned, by their labor, a share of whatever prosperity remained in the Old South. It was their Georgia, too. But the resistance imposed by the people in Lilly's world was as formidable as it was heartless. If the descendants of the slaves were going to rise above it all, Lilly thought, they would have to do it individually as well as collectively. She knew that they possessed a strength that sustained them. Did she have the strength to sustain herself in *her* troubles, she wondered. Would *she* be able to rise above it all?

Lilly talked no more about her present concern. There was something in her quiet, contemplative mood that kept Grace at a certain distance. They spent the late-summer days in Savannah in simple leisure, taking long walks on sunny mornings and reading under the shelter of the piazza roof on rainy afternoons. Grace understood, without asking, that Lilly would make her decision in her own time and in her own way.

Chapter 15

Ivan Moss was being beaten for the first time in his life. It had never happened to him in the boxing ring, or anywhere else. He had always been able to see his opponents. If they were not right in front of his face, he knew where to find them. Now he couldn't find anybody. There were people in New Orleans who owed him favors and who should have been able to help. They were either gone or working for someone else. Too many new people were moving in. Prohibition was turning even small-time crooks into big operators who could hook up with people all over the country. Everybody was making money and elbowing anyone weaker aside, but nobody had time to help a fat cat like Ivan Moss chase down his prey.

Mac Harrison was gone. That was all Ivan could find out. Where or when or with whom were questions that would probably never be answered. Ivan had to decide on his next move. He could go back to Tampa and wait, or he could act on the one good piece of information he had: he knew where to find Lilly Harrison. There were still plenty of people in Tampa who feared him. Small people—ticket sellers and porters—saw things that Mr. Moss needed to know and told him about it. They told him Mrs. Harrison had gone to Savannah with another young woman. It should be easy enough, Ivan finally decided. It was certainly easier than going back home and listening to his father's criticism.

There were several ways to perform the task now in front of him. He could find a place to wait and have someone else bring the woman to him. But Ivan Moss was tired of the obstacles. He decided to do things in a direct, uncomplicated way.

A week after he made his decision, he was standing at the front door of the address he had been given. Sunday morning had made his task even less complicated. Aunt Eunice and Grace, and the three house servants, had gone to church. He rang the bell and waited, not bothering to remove his hat, as would have been the custom of any friendly caller in Savannah. As Lilly approached the door and hesitated, Ivan pushed it open with one hand and grabbed her face with the other, muffling her screams as he shoved her down into a chair. "You keep your mouth shut," he said through clenched teeth, as he pushed his mouth against her ear. "You can settle up this thing with me, or I can break your neck right now."

All of Lilly's instincts made her want to fight, to flail away with everything she had, but her reason prevailed. In the midst of her fear, she caught the meaning of his words. She could calm down, she thought, and deal with this problem now, and perhaps even end it. She nodded her head and waited for Ivan to release his hold.

"Please. I know what you want," she said, her pounding heart almost taking away her breath. "Please don't hurt me. I don't know where Mac is, but he's not here, and wherever he is, I don't think he's coming back."

"I don't know where he is either, lady, and I don't care anymore. I just want my money. If you're like every other woman I know, then I'm sure you got most of what he took from me. Just give it to me, and I'll leave you alone."

"What makes you think you can get away with this," said Lilly, who was becoming emboldened by facing her fears. "Do you believe that you're completely immune from the law?"

"Don't talk to me like you're so innocent. You spent his money. You knew where it came from, and you didn't care, did you? I saw the jewelry he bought you. Now that the son of a bitch is gone, you think you can just forget about it. You think you can run to your daddy and tell him you didn't do anything wrong."

"I *do* just want to forget about it. How much money do I have to give you?"

"Mac owes me forty-thousand dollars."

"I thought it was thirty-two thousand."

Ivan Moss laughed and sat down on the sofa, putting his feet on the coffee table in front of him and folding his arms. He was enjoying the exchange of words with this woman; she was not the kind he dealt with every day. He knew that she felt herself to be superior to him, and he wanted to watch her humiliation when she realized that nothing she possessed was equal to the power he had. Everybody was afraid of his father, and he had learned to use that, to bring down the reality of that fear on anyone who stood in his way. This woman's family and refined speech meant nothing to him, no matter how much ordinary people were impressed by such things.

"So you aren't so innocent, are you?" Ivan continued. "If you know that much about it, then I guess you'll just have to take care of it."

"I don't have that much money. If I give you half of it, will you leave us alone?"

"Why do you say 'us'? I thought you said your husband wasn't coming back?"

"I mean my father and me. Will you leave my father and me alone if I give you fifteen-thousand dollars?"

"Half of thirty-two thousand is sixteen thousand."

"All right, for God's sake! I'll give you sixteen thousand. Please just let that be enough. I have to get beyond this trouble; I'm going to have a baby. I know that's not something you would care about, but please, you must have some shred of decency in you."

"You're right; it's not something I care about. I care about getting my money back. Wait a minute! What are you gonna do with a baby if you don't have a husband anymore?"

"What kind of question is that? It's none of your concern, anyway."

"Well, maybe I'm interested. Maybe I'm in the market for a baby. If it's Mac's, it should be a pretty good-looking kid—and you're a good-looking woman. Give me the sixteen thousand, and I'll wait until you have the kid. Nobody else is gonna give you that much."

Lilly tried to get up from the chair, but her legs trembled and her mind whirled in confusion and disbelief. For the first time, her instincts were centered on something other than her own well-being. The unborn child, whose emergence had created aversion and troubling doubts about the future, was now the most important thing in her life. In the midst of her fear and revulsion of Ivan Moss, she suddenly saw the life within her as real. It was a person—a person as dear to her as anyone else in her life, and the one who most needed her protection. This evil, which had started out as nothing more than a revealing confirmation of her doubts about her husband, was now reaching into her very soul, like the hand of Satan.

Ivan continued to talk, insensible of the horror and rejection with which his words were received. "Look, I know you don't want this thing, anyway. You ain't got no use for it. Nobody wants to hook up with a woman that's got somebody else's kid. I could use it. My wife can't have none; she's got somethin' wrong with her. I don't want everybody knowing that, or I would get one from the orphanage or somewhere. I can take yours. You just stay up here and have it. I'll come get it, and in the meantime, my wife can pretend she's pregnant—she can tie a pillow around her belly or somethin' like that." Ivan laughed and slapped Lilly on the back as he walked around her chair and continued with his plan. "Now you don't say nothin'. You understand? You keep your mouth shut about this. The only thing I want you to do is tell my wife that it's your kid and that Mac is the father. I don't want her thinkin' I knocked up some slut. She won't take it if she thinks that."

Lilly gradually regained her senses as Ivan continued to talk. All of her thoughts were focused on getting him out of the house. She was conscious of the mental advantage she held. She tried to calmly use this weapon without showing it to the man who was obviously distracted by his own words. She nodded in agreement at the first opening in his absurd speech. "Your right, Ivan; I don't really want the baby. Maybe this will work out, but you need to give me time to arrange things. Nobody knows I'm expecting, not even my father. My aunt and my friend will be home from church in just a few minutes, though. You better leave right away."

Ivan turned to leave but then turned back and pointed his finger at her. "You still gotta get me the money. Don't think cause I'll be your kid's father, that I'll forget the money. You get it together for me. You hear?"

The front door slammed shut. Lilly unclenched her fists and took a deep breath. Fear and doubt left her at that moment, and she saw clearly, for the first time, a fundamental truth about the human universe. Good and evil were real, and every person seemed to be, to a greater or lesser extent, an incarnation of either entity. No one is born evil, she thought, but people allow themselves to become that way in a blind search for power and money. Frank and Ivan Moss were embodiments of selfish greed—parasites who fed upon and infected every person who happened to come into their sphere. She wondered if Mac Harrison was really any different. The darker aspect of his nature had been hard to discover in the beginning, but perhaps it was cultivated and nourished by people whose capacity for evil was greater.

Lilly now understood that it was not their way of making a living that was evidence of their baseness. That aspect of their lives was wrong mainly in the sense that it violated artificial laws—laws that were sometimes as capricious as the politicians who wrote them. She, herself, had partaken of the bootlegged liquor with no real belief that it was sinful. The business of narcotics seemed on the surface to be no worse, but she had an idea of the destruction it caused in the people who were the ultimate source of its profits.

The true nature of wickedness, Lilly suddenly realized, could only be seen in the negative—in the absence of those qualities that reflected goodness in people. And those qualities all seemed to come down to selflessness. Kindness, sympathy, charity—even love itself—all were reflections of caring about others. The people close to her, the best people she knew, always seemed to have genuine hopes for her well-being. They cared about her happiness without considering a return for their efforts. They would share her joys, stand vigilantly with her against her fears, and ultimately, heal her sorrows. Papa would do all that, she thought. So would Grace and Evan.

"But what about me?" Lilly said out loud to herself. "Have I been selfish? Have I been so worried about myself that I haven't thought enough about them? Have I thought enough about this child growing inside me?"

Chapter 16

Nick Cancello was enjoying one of his favorite things. He was dancing cheek to cheek with a pretty young girl under a full moon. He cradled her waist in his right arm and playfully stroked her fingers as he held on to her hand and guided her gracefully around the dance floor. The band was playing just loudly enough to muffle the sharp sounds of a woman's high heel shoes striking the planks of the pier. Grace grabbed Nick from behind and twisted him away from his startled young partner. "Nicky, I need you right now!" she yelled above the music. "You've gotta help me, please. You gotta do something about that crazy bastard! How could you ever have a friend like that?"

Nick took Grace by the shoulders and firmly, but gently, walked her back across the dance floor and away from the noise of the music and the crowd. "Now settle down, toots," he said as he turned her around and studied her face under the moonlight. "Tell me what the hell you're talking about."

"Ivan—your friend Ivan—that's what I'm talking about."

"Grace, he's not my friend; he never was my friend. What's he done now?"

"I don't want to talk here, Nicky. Let's go sit in my car."

"No, we'll sit in *my* car. I'm not gonna be seen in that bucket of bolts you're driving."

They walked up the pier and down the gravel drive to a clump of ancient oak trees where Nick's roadster was parked. Nick opened the door for Grace and walked around the back of the car to the driver's side, sighing and turning up his palms in frustration during the few seconds he had alone. Grace began pouring out her story before the door was shut. "Nick, you're not gonna believe what's happened. Ivan found out that we were in Savannah. He came up there while Lilly was alone in the house. We just got back to Tampa this morning, and I've been looking for you all day."

Nick's expression instantly changed to a stony seriousness. He stared intently at Grace and listened to every word she said, exhaling slowly when he learned that Lilly was unhurt. "Grace, I'm sorry," he said earnestly. "I warned you and the judge about him. I was hoping he'd just stay after Mac for a while."

"You haven't heard the worst part yet, Nick. You've got to keep this to yourself, though. Lilly is pregnant."

"By who?"

"By Mac! Who do you think? You know Lilly; why would you ask such a thing? That goon wants her baby. He said he would take half the money Mac owes him, and then the baby when it's born. You don't look surprised, Nicky."

"Toots, nothing about Ivan Moss surprises me. The more money he's made, the more he thinks he can have anything he wants. It doesn't surprise me, either, that he wants a baby. I don't know if you heard the story, but it got around that he beat up his wife pretty bad one time. Ivan can be brutal. He probably punched her or kicked her in the stomach. If she can't have kids, that's something that Ivan would be upset about because I've heard his old man call him a pansy in front of other people. He would want a kid just to show it off."

"Nicky!" Grace shoved Nick in the chest with both hands and glared at him indignantly. "Why are you taking this so lightly? Lilly's my best friend—she's like my sister. Don't you see how horrible this is?"

"I know, toots," Nick answered, grabbing her wrists in a way that was more affectionate than defensive. "I'm not making light of anything. I'm just trying to tell you what this man is like. I know it's horrible, but everything about Ivan and his family is horrible. Believe me, I've seen some things I wish I'd never seen. If I had it all to do over again, I would have never gone anywhere near those people. I've spent the last two years trying to stay away from them, but Ivan still acts like I'm one of his buddies. But, Grace, I hope you believe me; I never did anything bad like they do. I just did a few stupid things, when I was younger, that I shouldn't have done."

"If I asked you to kill Ivan and his father, would that be a stupid thing?"

"Grace! Don't even think something like that." Nick opened the car door and looked around to see if anyone was close enough to have heard them talking.

Grace folded her arms and began to cry. "I don't know what else to do, Nicky. The whole time she was with Mac, I felt like I had lost her—like she had been taken away from me by that jerk. Now he's gone, but things are even worse. Lilly's scared to death—I know she is—but she's trying to act like she can get through it. She always wants to be strong like her mama. Can't you do something? She's staying with her brother and her father at the lake, but I'm still worried."

"I don't know, toots. I know I'm not gonna kill anybody, even for you. The best thing Lilly can do is to give Ivan the money as soon as she can. I don't know how much she has, but if he says he'll take sixteen thousand, then she needs to give it to him. Maybe he'll stay away from her awhile, at least until we can figure out what to do about this crazy idea he has. He probably won't do anything to hurt her if he really wants the baby. You never told me what Lilly thinks about the baby. Forgive me for asking this: Does she want to have it? I mean, does she want to keep it? You know what I mean?"

"Yes, Nick, she wants it. I don't really think she did at first, but I also don't think it was what Ivan did that changed her mind. She had kept pretty quiet about it, but I usually know what she's thinking. I believe she had already made up her mind to have it before Ivan came up there. She wasn't happy about it, though."

"You ever think about having children, Grace?"

"Sometimes. I would if I were married to somebody I really loved. My mama wants me to settle down; I can tell you that. I can also tell you that she's not too happy that I've been seen in your company a few times. But I like you, Nicky. You're certainly a much better man than Mac Harrison. I don't care how many war medals he has. In fact, I like you better than just about any of the men around here."

"I like you, too, Grace. I like you a lot. Sometimes I think I *could* kill somebody for you."

Chapter 17

Lilly was quiet on the ride from Union Station to the lake house where her father was waiting for her. Evan passed it off as just her fatigue from the trip. When they were almost there, she turned to her brother and prepared him for what he would hear. "I have a lot to say, Evan, but I can only say it once, I think. I hope you have nothing important to do right away, because I need to talk to you and Papa together."

Judge Jenkins heard Evan's car coming up the drive and got up from his desk in the new office his son had prepared for him in the east bedroom. He hugged his daughter for a long time, but he could tell she was impatient to tell him something.

"Papa, you and Evan need to sit down. Grace didn't come out here with me; she's still in town. She knows everything, of course, but I wanted to talk to you alone. I want to know how you feel about everything, and I want you to be able to speak freely. I'm going to have a baby. I've known about it for a while, but I didn't tell you because I wasn't sure what to do about it."

The conflicting thoughts in Lilly's father's mind came across his face as an arrested smile and then as a searching, bewildered look in his eyes. "Sugar, I—"

"Don't say anything yet, Papa. There's a lot I have to tell you. I didn't want it, Papa. I couldn't stand the thought of it. I couldn't bring myself to say anything to you because I was sure you wouldn't understand. I'm not sure you'll understand *now*, but so much has happened to me. It was going to be taken away from me. Something I didn't want was going to be taken away. Somebody evil—the most evil person I know—wants something that I didn't want—something that I was going to throw away."

Evan rose up from his chair with clenched fists and a red face. "Did Mac find you in Savannah? I swear, Lilly, if he doesn't stay away from you, I'll kill him."

Judge Jenkins pulled his chair closer to Lilly and held up his hand toward Evan, motioning for him to sit down. "Son, just settle down a bit," he said, with an impatience that Evan hadn't seen since childhood. "Sugar, what in the world is going on?"

"There's a lot going on, Papa, but the important thing is that I know what I need to do about everything. As I said, I didn't want the baby at first. I started feeling guilty, though, after I got to Aunt Eunice's. I was trying to find a way to justify not having it, but I just couldn't. Bessie Mae made me feel like a spoiled brat. I was trying to pretend that I was desperate, that I needed help, but that's ridiculous. She made me see that I'm not desperate at all; I've got my family and enough money to live a comfortable, happy life. But I still didn't really want to have it, not until I found out that Ivan Moss wanted to take it from me."

"Ivan Moss!" Evan and his father yelled it out at the same time.

"Yes, Papa. Somehow he found out where I was. He came to Aunt Eunice's and threatened me about the money."

Lilly's father got up and paced around the room, punching the door frame with the side of his fist as he walked past it. It was the first time his children had ever seen him strike at anything in anger. "Sugar, Eunice should have told me about this. She was responsible for your safety up there, and she can't even take the time to let me know what's happening to you?"

"She didn't know, Papa. I was alone in the house while she and Grace went to church. I told Grace, but I didn't want Aunt Eunice to know that somebody like that had been in her house. There's nothing she could have done about it, anyway, Papa."

"Lilly, did he lay a hand on you? Did he do anything to hurt you?" said Evan, who was sitting down now and trying to appear calm despite his rapid breathing and anxious eyes.

"No," Lilly lied, "he didn't touch me. He just threatened me. I thought I could appeal to his sympathy by telling him I was expecting. I was so foolish. I might just as well have expected sympathy from a rattlesnake. Now look what I've done: he wants the baby. I told him I didn't have all the money, and I offered to pay him half. He says he'll take the baby for the other half, and he doesn't seem to think I would have any problem with that at all. He was sure that I wouldn't want it. And the thing is, Papa, he was right. But in that second, when I thought it would be taken away from me by somebody like him, everything changed. I wouldn't give it up for anything now—not for anything, Papa. You've got to stop him. You have to find a way."

"Sugar, it's all my fault," said Lilly's father, shaking his head and trying to stop the beginnings of tears building up in his eyes "I should have done something about this a long time ago. I'm no different than everyone else around here, I guess. Everybody's afraid of these people, but I was ashamed to admit that *I* was. I tried to justify my unwillingness to act right away by my concern for our reputation. That's meaningless to me now. If the people in this town can change their good opinion of me because of the low character of my son-in-law, then I want nothing to do with them. The only thing that matters to me is your safety. I'm happy that you're going to have a baby. I know it's not going to be under ideal circumstances, sugar, but at least Mac won't be around—at least I hope not—to influence this child."

"You're really happy about it, Papa? That's what I wanted to know."

"Of course, sugar. Why wouldn't I be? You should remember that my papa died when I was only two years old. I don't remember him at all. I grew up well enough without a father around, but if he had been killed in the war, I wouldn't be here. None of us would be here. I think of all the bullets that must have passed so close to him. Somehow, they all missed. So you see, our existence is miraculous. If you choose not to have this child, you would be negating a miracle."

Lilly's father walked out of the bedroom door and out onto the side porch. He stood there for a moment before walking down the steps and out under the grape arbor. He pulled a few muscadine grapes from the vine above his head, and continued walking down to the lakeshore. Lilly sat quietly with Evan and watched her father walk out to the dock.

"What do you think he will do?" asked Lilly. "I don't want him to put himself in any danger."

"Lilly, Papa has had to deal with bad characters before. As I see it, there are really only two things that can be done. Either we pay the Moss family all of the money, or we go to the police chief and ask to have them arrested. Paying the money would be the simplest way to end this, but I'm not sure Papa can do that."

"You don't think so, Evan?" Lilly asked, with more than a little surprise. "I know Papa isn't rich, but when he gave Mac and me the money at our wedding, he said that it wouldn't be a strain on him. He said he had done well on the land that he bought with Uncle Oliver and Aunt Maggie."

"He thought he had done well, Lilly. I've found out a lot of things since I've been helping him with the new practice. They didn't have a clear title to that land. The land company turned out to be as crooked as a dog's hind leg. They lost everything. I think the worst part about it is that Papa feels so bad about Aunt Maggie losing her money. Papa trusted Uncle Oliver; he never thought it would be necessary to look more closely into everything. Aunt Maggie went into it because of Papa."

"You mean to tell me he's broke? I can't believe that."

"He's not broke, but sixteen thousand is about five thousand more than he has. He gave Aunt Maggie several thousand to make up for her loss. He's standing out there on the dock for a reason I think he's probably trying to think of what to say to Chief Davis."

Chapter 18

1921 had been an interesting year for Leland Davis. There were so many laws being broken that he spent most of his time trying to figure in which direction to deploy his force. Young people seemed to have so much energy now. They were speeding around town, sometimes drunk, but always following a crowd out to have a good time. Prohibition didn't seem to stop anybody from drinking, he thought, except for a few hen-pecked husbands of church matrons. As far as he was concerned, it was the federal agents' job to worry about the liquor. He had his hands full just trying to keep people from killing each other, or from disturbing the peace with their boisterous jazz music. There were larger problems going on, and they usually involved organized criminals fighting with their enemies, or fighting among themselves. He knew that this lawyer coming to see him today had a serious problem, and though he didn't know the details, he suspected that it involved his son-in-law.

Chief Davis greeted his visitor in his usual cold and officious manner. "I've got a few minutes, Mr. Jenkins. I understand you have something that you wanted to see me about. I'm aware that people call you Judge Jenkins. I'm not sure why. You've never been a judge around here, have you?"

"Well, no, sir, I haven't. I was a county judge in Georgia. I suppose people just picked up on that somehow from my family and friends who moved down here ahead of me. Other people heard them call me that, and it just sort of stuck, I guess."

"Well, you won't mind, then, if I just call you Mr. Jenkins. I have to address enough people around here as Judge, and since you're not really one, anyway, I don't think I should have to extend that courtesy to you if it's not deserved."

Lilly's father was more amused than offended. "Certainly, Chief, you just call me whatever you want. As the colored people back home would say, '*I ent hab no use to be laa'gin*'. That is, I don't have any reason to make myself bigger than I am."

"Well, Mr. Jenkins, I have an idea of why you're here. Your son-in-law is someone we kept an eye on. I know he's been gone for some time, so I suspect he's caused you some trouble."

"I must say, I'm surprised, Chief Davis. He is, in fact, the cause of my troubles, but I was unaware that he had drawn your notice."

"It's my duty to notice people, Mr. Jenkins. Mr. Harrison was somewhat of a loudmouth, if you know what I mean. He drew attention to himself on several occasions, and he was involved in activities that he should have wanted to keep quiet about."

"I presume then, Chief, that you know who he associated with."

"Yes."

Judge Jenkins waited for an elaboration that never came. He broke the silence mainly for the purpose of ending the police chief's irritating stare. "Then you have an idea of the nature of my trouble. Frank Moss and his son are threatening my family, my daughter in particular."

"Mr. Jenkins, that's the outcome of associating with people you don't know. I would think that the family members of a respectable lawyer would want to keep to their own society."

Judge Jenkins tried to stay calm, but he felt his face reddening. "Chief Davis, Mr. Harrison, as far as I'm concerned, is no longer a member of my family. We want nothing to do with these people. We want to be left alone, and we expect the police department to protect us. You have no idea what this man Ivan is threatening to do."

"Oh, I have an idea, Mr. Jenkins. But again, this is a problem of associating with people outside your circle. Nobody broke into your daughter's house and tried to steal from her or tried to assault her. Isn't that correct?"

"He broke into my sister's house in Savannah. He may not have touched my daughter, but I'm sure his actions came up to the level of assault."

"Well, that sounds like a matter for the Savannah Police Department, doesn't it? If you were a judge up there, you should know who to contact."

Judge Jenkins used all the years of his experience in court to try to understand the man in front of him. The possible motives for such irrational obstinacy were unsettling. He took a deep breath and tried to remain calm. "It's obvious to me, Mr. Davis, that you have no inclination at all to help me. I don't know if the power of these people is such that it overwhelms local authority, or if it's just a case of your own interests interfering with the performance of your duties. I suppose I can appeal to a higher authority, but God knows how high this man's reach extends. I at least have a right to defend my family. As a lawyer, I know that to be a fact. Do I have to worry about you interfering with that?"

"I'm not gonna interfere with you unless you give me reason to, Mr. Jenkins. I understand that you've split with your partners and that you're practicing out in the county. That's probably a good place for you. Tampa's not Savannah; the people around here know their place. Your son-in-law didn't know any better, but you should be smarter than that. If he's in some financial obligation, he needs to settle it. If that obligation has fallen on your shoulders, you need to do the same. As far as making accusations against anyone in this town, remember that it's almost impossible to tar someone without getting tar on yourself."

Judge Jenkins saw no good purpose in continuing this frustrating verbal contest. He left the chief's office in as cold a manner as he had been received, something that went against everything in his nature and breeding. As much as he hated to admit it, there was some truth in Leland Davis's advice. Paying off these hoodlums would be the sensible thing, he thought. He had counted up the amount of his resources in his head a dozen times. It still came up the same. By his reckoning, the cash in his bank, combined with what he knew Lilly had, was enough, but it would wipe them out. He knew that he would have to decide very soon whether or not to take this drastic step. He wanted to get his family out of danger and let Lilly have her child in peace.

A meeting with Nick Cancello had been arranged in the judge's old law office. Nick was there waiting, along with Grace, when Lilly's father walked in. "Well, my goodness, I see that it's your turn to bring a pretty, blonde lady to a meeting," Judge Jenkins said smiling, some of his natural good humor having returned.

"She just followed me in, Judge," said Nick with mock bewilderment. "She's been following me around a lot lately. I can't even go to a dance without her finding me."

Grace ignored the teasing and took over the conversation. "Judge, did Lilly tell you everything. I told her she had to. I told her to talk to you and Evan both, as soon as she got out there."

"She did. Now, I have a question for you. Did my sister know anything about what happened up there? Lilly told me she didn't."

"That's the truth. Lilly didn't want to upset her. That's the thing about Lilly, Judge. She's always worried about everybody else. You could cut off her arm, and she would be worried about getting blood on your floor. I know she has her limit, though. I've only seen her reach it a few times, but it's pretty scary when she does."

"Well, I've reached *my* limit, sugar. I just left the police station and I found out that we're not going to get any help from Chief Davis."

"Gee, I could have told you that, Judge," said Nick, shaking his head. "I could've saved you the trip. See, you never had any dealings with him involving these kinds of people. You only saw him in court when it had something to do with your clients, and most of your clients were quality people. I was the only bad apple you ever represented."

This drew an elbow from Grace and a laugh from Lilly's father. "I had worse than you, Nick. Some of these people you call quality are the biggest crooks in town. There are all kinds of ways to steal from people, and hurt people. What you did was nothing much, but I know you're sorry about it, anyway. You're a good man, Nick. I'm pretty sure about that."

The young man accepted the compliment in silence, then repeated the advice he had given to Grace. "Judge, you're just gonna have to pay these people. I don't see any way around it. They think Lilly was right in with Mac on this stuff. They're not gonna let her go. The best way to get Ivan off this crazy idea about the baby is to just give him all the money. They've got other things to do. Believe me, they'll go away if they think they've squared things up."

"Nick, that's all I want them to do. I want them to go away. If you can do a favor for me, I would be deeply grateful to you. I want you to take the money to them. They wouldn't see anything unusual in that, would they?"

"No, I don't think so, Judge. They don't have anything against *me*. I don't like them, but they don't know that because I know how to talk to them. I know what to say and what not to say. They've seen me around town with Grace, and they've seen Lilly with her. They wouldn't be surprised that I was asked to do something like that. I'm not gonna say hardly anything, though. I'm just gonna hand them the money and tell them who it's from."

"Can I go with you, Nicky," said Grace. "I won't be any trouble; I just want to let that goon know that I'm not afraid of him."

"Toots, are you crazy? I wouldn't trust you around him for a minute. I think you're the greatest thing in the world, but you don't know how to keep your mouth shut. That's not just a criticism of *you*; I would say that about *any* woman."

"Now take it easy, kids," said the judge, holding up his hands. "Grace, I'm not going to defend Nick on that last point, but you're not going anywhere near Ivan Moss. After Nick walks out of here today, I don't want another word said about any of these people. I'll deal with whatever legal issues arise concerning the marriage, but that's about it. You need to take care of your friend. I want her to stay out there where Evan and I can keep an eye on her, but you're certainly welcome to come out and stay as long as you want. Nick, I know you're a city boy, but you come out and see us when you can. Maybe Evan can teach you to fish. My goodness, I just want life to get back to normal. It hasn't been normal since Elizabeth died."

Chapter 19

The money was gathered together. The hardest thing for Lilly's father was asking his daughter to give up her dowry. But there was no other way. They were each left with about a thousand dollars, and they would live together on the income from the small country law practice. Lilly urged her father to go back to his old firm in town, but he would have none of it. "I wouldn't be any use to them," he said. "My mind would be here with you. You know, your mother's death took me away from here, and I can't help thinking that if I had stayed, everything would be different."

But Lilly knew that it wasn't true. Mac would have been able, she thought, to continue his plans right under her father's nose. The only thing that could have changed was her resistance. Perhaps her father's presence would have given her courage or, at least, embarrassed her enough to put a stop to the whole mess.

Nick Cancello believed he was doing his part to put an end to it. He went directly to Frank Moss. He had told

Grace that he wanted to make sure there was nothing else he didn't know about. Moss eyed him intently, but not really suspiciously, when he stated the reason for his visit. The older man's mind worked in a straightforward fashion. To him, the balance sheet had been reconciled, and the power of the fear he created in anyone attempting to oppose him had been proven. He motioned for Nick to sit down while he examined the contents of the bag and made a mental note to himself to bludgeon any further signs of cockiness emanating from his less-than-worthy son. Nick looked on in disgust, his expression unseen by the man who was absorbed in counting his money. It was more money, the young man thought, than he would ever have in his life.

Nick went straight from Frank Moss to Grace. The short trip was symbolic. He was leaving, he hoped for the last time, all connections with his past. The money paid wasn't for him, but it felt like it. It felt like it was buying his freedom. He knew that he wasn't one of these people, that he was a good person, and that he could have a good life with somebody like Grace.

He had never met anyone like her. She was feminine, but she could be as tough as any guy he knew. She was never mean or spiteful, but she let everybody know that she couldn't be pushed around. He liked her happy, carefree manner, and he liked her independent streak, too. It was the first thing he had noticed about her. He had seen her driving around town in that Model T, always by herself or with Lilly. He hoped she would appreciate and understand what he had done for her. From the first day, when he had taken her by the arm and warned her about Ivan Moss, he had hoped that Lilly's father would do the smart thing and get rid of these people.

Nick wanted to start life in a new place, maybe outside of town where he wouldn't have to pass people like Ivan Moss on the street. He wanted to tell Grace about his plan. He had talked her out of her Model T and into his roadster on one occasion, already. Maybe he could convince her to make it a permanent change.

Convincing Mrs. Morgan would be the hardest thing. She opened the door and tried to make her smile look natural and genuine. She failed miserably, but after Nick returned her greeting in his likable, courteous way, she began to soften a little. He certainly was a fine looking man; she had to admit that. She would try to accept Judge Jenkins' favorable opinion of him, at least until she could see some proof to the contrary, but after being fooled by Captain Harrison, Mrs. Morgan's confidence in her ability to make good judgments of people was somewhat shaken.

Grace almost flew down the stairs when she heard Nick's voice. They went straight to the front porch and sat in the swing, where Grace and Lilly had spent so many evenings talking about things they didn't want anyone else to hear. "I think it's over, toots," said Nick. "If there was anything else we had to worry about, Frank Moss would have said so. I know it cost them a lot, but Lilly and her father need to forget about all this. That's exactly what I'm going to do."

Grace took Nick's hand and leaned her head on his shoulder. "Thanks for everything, Nicky. This has been such a battle, and having you around has really helped. Lilly's father is a very smart man, but I think he needed someone like you to make him understand what he was up against."

"Do you still want to have me around? I don't have any more dragons to kill for you, but maybe I could entertain you, at least."

"Yeah, I want you around. There's a question I have, though. The night I came to find you at the pier, you were dancing with someone. Who was she?"

"Just some girl from St. Pete. I can't remember her name."

"You certainly looked like you were enjoying yourself. You didn't look like you needed to wait around for some little lost girl like me to come back from Georgia."

"Toots, there may be a few little lost girls in this town, but you're not one of them. If you were, I wouldn't be interested. And I *did* think about you while you and Lilly were gone. As a matter of fact, I thought about some things I wanted to say to you. The first thing is a question. Do you think your mother will ever get to where she doesn't look at me like a rat that needs killing?"

Grace laughed for the first time in weeks. "Don't worry about Mama, Nicky. She grew up in a little town in South Carolina, and the only Italians she knew about were the ones in Shakespeare. She just needs to get to know you. Papa likes everybody, so he won't be a problem for you. What else did you want to tell me?"

"Well, I've been making some plans. There's a place for sale on Lake Bonita. That's where the old Chinaman used to live, the one who knew so much about the oranges. Anyway, it's not too far from Lilly's place, and I thought if I could buy it, you might want to come out and visit me. I think I can make a good living with citrus. You know, Sicilians are pretty good at growing things."

Grace didn't answer right away, but by the way her feet were swaying back and forth beneath the swing, Nick could tell she was thinking. "Just to visit?" she asked, in a voice he could barely hear.

"Well, toots, there's an old barn still there. There's plenty of room to park your Model T. It'll be out of the weather, and it won't be in anybody's way."

Grace squeezed Nick's hand. They had answered each other's questions. After a few minutes of silence, and a few kisses, Grace talked about something else that was on her mind. "Nicky, I'm gonna have to spend a little time with Lilly. I fought so hard for her to have this baby. I need to help her as much as I can. Her papa and Evan are wonderful, but she needs a woman around for this. I'm going to be the godmother, anyway, so I need to be there."

"I know, Gracie; we can both look after her. I can be the *padrino,* if there are no other candidates. My grandmother used to tell me that in Sicily, the *padrinos* were supposed to keep enemies away from the family. I've already done that. I've tried to, anyway."

Chapter 20

Early-morning fog spread across the lake and drifted above the grass on the west lawn. An occasional, far-away sound of a bass striking the surface of the water, and the nearer sounds of late-summer guavas falling from the trees beside the house, were the only noises which could awaken anyone sleeping on this Sunday morning.

Lilly felt the hand across her face, and in the few lucid moments following, she was aware of the ether filling her nose and lungs. Her struggle was brief and futile. The man cradled her limp body in his arms and carried her through the bedroom door and out onto the porch. With little effort, and unusual agility, he stepped down to the ground, avoiding the creaking steps as he had done on his way in. He could have saved himself the trouble. Lilly's father and brother knew that she was always up before the sun. They had grown accustomed to doorknobs being gently turned in the darkness, and the sound of steps lightly taken on wooden floors.

Once the man was on the ground, he walked steadily and tirelessly for almost a quarter of a mile to the car he had parked behind a clump of palmettos down the road. He dragged Lilly in through the passenger door. After he got behind the wheel, he laid her head on his lap and steered the car out to the road. He headed north on the winding country highway, planning in his head the route he would take out of Florida.

An hour later, the sun had come up fully and was shining through the trees around the lake. Evan walked down to the dock for the third time. He looked along the lakeshore in both directions, hoping to see Lilly walking among the ferns and cypress knees, or throwing pieces of bread to the fish at the mouth of the creek. He swallowed hard and tried to control the panic rising in his chest. He searched his mind for an explanation and quickly discounted the likelihood of her going off with Grace. The rattling Model T would have awakened them all.

He hurried back to the house, dreading more than anything the task of informing his father of such a disturbing event as Lilly's unexplained absence. Evan opened the bedroom door just as his father was waking up. There was nothing to do but spit out the words. "Papa, I can't find Lilly. I've looked all over."

Lilly's father threw the sheet aside and searched frantically for his glasses, as if he had to see clearly the source of the words to believe them. "What in God's name do you mean, Son? I saw her go to bed last night."

"I know, Papa; I did too. I thought I heard her in the kitchen. I was going out to have coffee with her, but she wasn't there. She's never in bed after daylight, so I looked in on her. Her bed's not made, either. She always makes it as soon as she gets up."

The ominous words, combined with Evan's frightened tone and expression, made his father's heart sink. Judge Jenkins' rational mind told him there had to be a benign explanation, but just the very thought of something happening to her shook him to his core. He tried to get his bearings, and he thought of the previous day's meeting with Nick. He had gone to bed hopeful of the outcome of his decision to pay Lilly's tormentors. He had even been optimistic about the loss of the money. He could earn enough in the new practice, he thought. They didn't live high like so many of the people in town; there would be more than enough to provide a good home for his daughter and grandchild. All of a sudden, he felt that his life was slipping away. He had awakened to tragic loss in this house for the second time.

Judge Jenkins had grown up in a world without telephones. He had not really minded not having one here at the lake, even though his friend's and relatives in town were coming to rely on them. He would have given anything to have one now, but all he could do was to instruct Evan to wait at the house while he drove into town. He would try the Morgans' house, even though it seemed unlikely that she would be there. Before leaving, he reluctantly handed the shotgun to his son. "Look around for her," he said, sighing heavily, "but don't go far from the house. I'll either come back and get you or send someone."

Evan had never heard his father curse or cry. He was doing both as he slammed the car door shut.

An hour later, Judge Jenkins was sitting in the Morgans' front parlor. Grace was crying and wringing her hands as she paced around the room. "God, where is Nick? He should have been here by now." Just as she got the words out, a car lunged into the driveway, the door opening and closing almost instantly. Nick bounded onto the porch, taking the four steps in one stride. As he entered the house, he heard Dr. Morgan telling Lilly's father that the police chief was on his way over.

Grace buried her head in Nick's chest. He stroked her hair while he spoke to Judge Jenkins. "Judge, all the way over here, I tried to sort this out in my head. Do you think Mac could have come during the night and taken her away? I just can't believe the Moss family would have anything to do with this. They don't operate like that. Anyway, I can't see any reason for it; they have their money. The old man acted just as I expected he would when I handed it to him."

"That was going to be my first question to you, Nick. You did give him the money, then. It's not that I didn't trust you; I've just been trying to figure this out myself. I don't know what to say about Mac. If he did do something like that, I wouldn't know where to find him. You know where Frank Moss is, though. If the police won't go there, you and I will have to."

Nick briefly considered this idea and then decided to change the subject. He didn't want to say just yet that it would be the wrong thing to do. "Do you want me here when the chief comes in, Judge? I don't believe he likes me very much."

"Stay right where you are, Nick. I don't like him very much, either."

Nick guided Grace over to the sofa and sat beside her. He had never felt as sorry for anyone in his life. She was shaking like a child, and he could tell that her natural strength of will had been overcome by grief.

They sat silently while Mrs. Morgan poured them some coffee. In a few minutes, Dr. Morgan showed Chief Davis and two policemen into the house. Nick left his place on the sofa and waited in the hallway. Judge Jenkins didn't get up. He held the coffee cup in his lap and glared at the chief for a full ten seconds before he spoke. "Is this what I had to wait for, Chief? Did I have to wait until my daughter was abducted from her own home before I could ask the city for help?"

Chief Davis pulled a chair from under the dining-room table and placed it in front of the sofa. He exhaled deeply before beginning to speak in a measured, even tone. "Mr. Jenkins, I'm not gonna get into an argument with you in a situation like this. You're understandably upset this morning. I don't believe you've thought this out, though. I came over here at Dr. Morgan's request, but this is not a matter for the City of Tampa. You live in the county. I'll be glad to call the sheriff's office for you."

Judge Jenkins leaned forward and looked Leland Davis directly in the eye. "Frank and Ivan Moss live in the city," he said flatly. "They may have had something to do with this. You know them better than the sheriff does and you have easier access to them. Unless you are an employee of theirs, which I don't believe is out of the question, I expect you to do something."

Dr. Morgan came quickly across the room at this last statement and put his hand on his friend's shoulder. "Now, Judge, try to contain yourself," he said. "You need help; you're not going to get it that way."

Chief Davis decided to speak only to Dr. Morgan. "Sir, I understand that this man is upset. I'll ignore his words, but if you want to help him, I suggest you take him to see Sheriff Turner, or better yet, he needs to turn his attention to his son-in-law. If his daughter left with anyone, my best guess is Mr. Harrison."

Lilly's father kept his head down while Chief Davis walked out of the room. On his way out the door, the chief stopped as he passed Nick. He stood only inches from the young man's face, in the way he had learned to do in years of police work, and spoke barely above a whisper. "Cancello, you've come up in the world. It seems trouble follows you, though, doesn't it?"

It took everything Nick had to remain silent, but he turned his head and took a deep breath and waited for Grace's father to escort the policemen out of the house. Grace walked out behind them. She paced back and forth in front of the house, her arms tightly folded against her, ignoring Nick's pleas to come back inside.

Nick returned to the parlor and sat down next to Lilly's father. The distraught man's head was still down, his hand covering his eyes. Nick spoke quietly to him and told him about his plan. "I know a few places where Mac might be likely to go if he's in town. I'm going to take a ride around, but you need to stay here. The sheriff will need to know where to find you if he's going to help us. I've been thinking about this, though. I don't know Mac all that well, but I can't understand why he would abduct his own wife. You know Lilly better than anybody. Would she leave with him at her own will?"

"Oh God, Nick, not in a million years. Even if she wanted to go with him, she wouldn't upset us like that."

Mrs. Morgan came rushing into the room, her normally placid face replaced by an expression of panic.

"Grace just left in her car, Judge. Her father tried to follow her, but he can't get *his* car started. She said she was going to the docks to find Frank Moss or his son. Somebody has to go after her, please!"

Nick moved as quickly as he could without knocking over everything in his path. As he made his way to his car, he berated himself under his breath for not keeping his eye on Grace. He had seen her riled up before, but he should have known that the reason for her anger now would push her to do anything.

Grace was ready to do anything. She was tired of watching these men sit by and argue while her best friend was missing. It was time to move, to drive as fast as she could, to find the people responsible for this and confront them. She didn't know if Frank Moss had anything to do with it or not, but she saw no reason for not finding out immediately. She had only a vague idea of the location of his office, but the adrenaline pumping through her veins sharpened her senses and her memory.

A sign on the side of a building, *Century Imports,* was suddenly familiar. Grace came to a screeching halt and backed up the car. She parked beside a stack of wooden pallets and got out, slamming the door as hard as she could to announce her arrival.

The only sign of life in the warehouse was a light burning in the small office at the top of the stairs. She hurried up the groaning staircase, hoping that the sound of her approach would disturb the man she was looking for. She wanted him to get up from whatever he was doing so that she could confront him directly—so that she could look straight into his vile face and tell him that she was not afraid—that if he had Lilly, she was here to take her back.

She was surprised that she was unchallenged as she reached the landing and knocked on the office door. The door wasn't completely closed, and the force of her knock pushed it open—until it was stopped by the body of Frank Moss.

Grace screamed at the sight of the bloody face staring vacantly in her direction. Her heart pounded and her ears rang with a second rush of adrenaline, but she gradually steadied herself and began walking as quickly as she could down the staircase.

Then, out of nowhere, Nick was at her side, flushed and out of breath from his race to catch up to her. "What in God's name are you doing, Grace?" he asked, in an angry tone he had never used with her before. "Do you want to get killed?"

Grace's lips were quivering too hard to form words. She took Nick's hand and pulled him up the staircase. As they reached the landing, a voice shouted from the open bay door. Chief Davis and one of his officers walked in with their guns drawn. They handcuffed Nick and pulled the small pistol from his pocket.

Chapter 21

"He was carrying a gun, Mr. Jenkins. I saw him at the bottom of the stairs as we got out of the car. If you think that doesn't decisively point to him as the murderer of Mr. Moss, then I don't know how in the world you practiced law all these years." Leland Davis said these words while glaring across his desk at Judge Jenkins, his face frozen in a mask of self-satisfaction and taunting superiority. "Nick Cancello was a punk kid, and that's what kids like that turn into. They turn into murderers and robbers."

"Nicky's not a murderer!" screamed Grace, whose swollen eyes and flushed face made her almost unrecognizable. The fear and sense of loss, which had nearly incapacitated her two hours ago, had now turned to rage. "I don't care about that filthy old man, anyway. I'm glad he's dead, but he was already dead when I got there. Nicky was just trying to help us find Lilly. That's all I care about, and you're not doing anything!"

Judge Jenkins had no ability—and no desire—to control Grace's outburst. When she finished, he calmly continued with what he had to say, realizing that getting to the truth of Frank Moss's death would help him find his daughter. "Listen to me, Chief Davis; I wasn't born yesterday, and despite your seeming lack of respect for me and my career, I've had plenty of experience with murderers. Nick had no motive whatsoever to kill this man. In fact, he told me that he had an amiable meeting with him last night."

"Let me stop you right there, Mr. Jenkins. He had a big motive. I'm sure he's done everything in the world to impress this girl, and now he thinks he's done the topper: he's killed the bad man for her. I don't know why she wants to protect this tally; she's from a respectable family. And the thing about tallies is they're so stupid they think they can get away with anything."

Grace knew that the tight squeeze of her arm was a plea for her to remain silent. She closed her eyes and willed herself to be quiet while Judge Jenkins answered the hurtful remarks. "I know Nick Cancello as well as anyone. He's a bright, decent young man. He's been a great help to me, and I consider him to be my friend. As I would with any friend, I will not allow him to be denigrated in my presence, and certainly not in such a vulgar way. This lady beside me is my daughter's best friend. I expect you to treat her with respect. If you can't do that, then you are no gentleman, and you have no business at all occupying the position you hold."

Leland Davis was unmoved by such remarks. He simply folded his arms and stared until the tension was relieved by a knock at his office door. One of the officers who had accompanied him earlier came in to the room. "You told me to let you know what we found, Chief," he said excitedly. "Well, Gorman dug one of the bullets out. It's the same as the rounds in Cancello's piece. But his pistol was full. Another thing, too: Doc says the body's stiff as a board; he didn't get shot this morning."

The chief said nothing as he opened his desk drawer and took out a cigar. It was almost as if the heavy puffs of smoke that poured out as he lit it were intended as a curtain to hide his thoughts. "I'm keeping him in jail, at least over night," he said from behind the smoky swirls. "He was there. I can keep him until I get all my questions answered." Leland Davis's eyes suddenly lit up. He took another puff on his cigar before putting it down. "I must be getting old," he said. "What did you just tell me? Cancello was there last night? That almost got right past me. I reckon you want to just kick yourself for disclosing that little bit of news, *Judge* Jenkins. You should be glad we're nailing this punk; it takes suspicion away from *you*. Some people would say *you* had a motive. I'm smart enough to know better—to know not to waste my time with you. This should be fun to watch, though. You have a little conflict of interest, it seems, in defending this guy."

Lilly's father stood up, locking his eyes on the mocking face of the police chief. "What kind of man are you?" he said, his voice breaking from anger. "There's no reason for you to be battling with me. I'm going through a horrible ordeal, and I need to know the truth behind it. I'll find the truth, I promise you, but I know I won't find it here. I want to see Nick right now. And I'm telling you, Davis, you better do all you can to help find my daughter.

If you don't, I'll have to talk to the mayor, or even the governor. Frank Moss is dead. If he had everyone in this state so goddamned scared, they ought to be happy today."

Judge Jenkins escorted Grace to her father's waiting car. It was all he could do to maintain his composure as he watched them drive away. He needed to stop and think for a moment, to focus his thoughts on what he had to do. He would be no help at all to Lilly, he thought, if he couldn't get his emotions under control.

He had already made a mistake in disclosing Nick's visit to Frank Moss. The police and prosecutor would put all of their attention on that fact and exclude everything else. The truth of Lilly's disappearance would be hidden in the things they would ignore. Judge Jenkins was sure that he knew the truth about Nick—almost sure, anyway.

He went back into the police station and waited for an intolerable amount of time before he was allowed to see his client. Nick began blurting out his defense before the guard even had a chance to open the cell door. "Judge, this is a load of crap. They got there two minutes after I did, and they're not that stupid; they didn't smell any smoke or anything. Hell, that's the first thing I noticed after the scare wore off. My gun was cold as ice, too. I shouldn't have been carrying the damn thing, but it's an old habit."

Judge Jenkins had always been a calm and rational person, and he had a certain way of calming everyone in his presence. He placed his hand on the young man's shoulder and motioned for him to sit down. He then took a few seconds to gather his thoughts before he began.

"They know that now, Nick. The coroner has already determined that Mr. Moss wasn't killed this morning. But they know that you met with him last night, and the coroner's report will probably say that was the time of his death. What do you think, Nick? Who should they be looking for?"

Nick ignored the questions. "How do they know I was there last night?"

"I'm afraid I told them, Nick. From a legal standpoint, it wasn't a smart thing to do, but unfortunately, my mind wasn't working too well. I'm sure you can understand why. But the truth will come out, Nick. It must come out—for your sake as well as Lilly's. Again, who should they be looking for?"

"They might want to look for Ivan's body, first. I already told them that. They said he wasn't home, but his car wasn't at the warehouse, either. I wouldn't be surprised if it's found on the causeway, or in the water—with him in it." Nick stared at the floor and shook his head. "Boy, somebody would have to be bold as hell to just walk in and shoot the old man like that."

"You know what I'm after, Nick. Do you think this is why Lilly is missing?"

"Yeah, Judge, I do. I thought I had evened things up last night, but evidently somebody's still out of whack. In my mind, that can only be Lilly's husband. He was a big war hero, I hear. I'm sure he's killed a lot of people before. What was that car your son-in-law drove? A Packard, was it? You need to tell that sorry-ass police chief to have everybody look for a Packard. If they don't find Ivan's Cadillac, with his body in it, they need to look in the trunk of Mac's car."

"Where would they look for Lilly?"

Nick could see the fear in Lilly's father's eyes, and he wanted more than anything else to say something to comfort him. "She would be in the front seat with him, Judge. She's safe. He doesn't have any reason to hurt her or his baby. She's safe, Judge. She's safe."

Chapter 22

As the car lumbered northward, to a destination not yet known to the driver, another ether-soaked handkerchief was placed over Lilly's face. The man had many things to say to her, but he wasn't ready. Later on, at a place of his choosing, he would bring her around and let her know about his plans. Lilly was aware only of a rushing sound, and then, very bright light. She sensed movement and was suddenly conscious of being in danger. The darkness came again, however, and the sickening fumes began to engulf her. She was being pulled down a long tunnel, as a high-pitched noise echoed in her head. The cycle was repeated over and over again. There was no sense of time or space but, incredibly, a heightened sense of self.

The light appeared again and got brighter and clearer. There was no noise and no movement. Lilly was aware now of being wrapped in coarse cloth, and as she tried to focus her vision, her body convulsed violently, and she vomited. A hand seized her by the nape of the neck and forced her head down over the edge of a bed. The same sickening smell of the fumes now seemed to pour out of her mouth and her nose.

A door opened, and an unfamiliar voice filled the room. "My goodness, Mister, your wife is certainly ill. Are you sure you don't want me to call a doctor? My wife is in the office. She's not a nurse, but she's had a lot of experience tending to the kids. I could go and fetch her for you, if you want."

Lilly coughed violently as she aspirated some of the liquid coming up in her throat. She could hear the door closing and the footsteps of the proprietor as he walked away, but not the answer to his offer. He was the only one who could help her now. The people who loved her, whose lives were torn apart by her disappearance, were hundreds of miles away. And they had been stunned and distracted by the murder of Frank Moss.

Lilly's father had recovered from his initial confusion. If he was going to save his daughter, he would have to use every talent he had. He would have to step away from his personal involvement with this case and look at the facts objectively. He had read the faces of hundreds of accused men in his life. Nick's expression was one of innocence, he believed. He would have reached that conclusion even if he had never met the man before.

There was one central idea that Lilly's father held on to. No matter what anyone else believed, he was convinced that the evil creature who had invaded his home and abducted his daughter was the murderer of Frank Moss. That fact had to eliminate Nick.

If only the seeds of doubt hadn't been planted. They came from the most unlikely source. "He said he had no more dragons to kill for me," Grace had told him. After a night's rest and a partial recovery from her shock, she had tearfully recounted their conversation on the porch swing. And even more troubling, was her disclosure of the final affirmative answer to her flippant request that night at the pier.

But Grace was after the truth as much as anyone else. Although she believed that she was in love with Nick, and that she would have stood with him against any attack, under any other circumstance, there was only one thing Grace wanted. If the proof of Nick's innocence could bring back her friend, that would be wonderful, but the proof of his guilt could do the same.

Judge Jenkins did everything he could to turn Grace's thoughts in the right direction. They walked together to the jail the next morning. The walk took them across the Hillsborough River, over the same bridge he had crossed with Lilly on the day this ordeal had begun. "Let's stop a moment, sugar," he said. They sat on a stone bench near the bridge tender's house. He could tell that Grace had wrapped herself in a numbing cloak of self-defense, and he wanted to make one last effort to get through to her.

"This is all hard for me," he began. "Even crossing this bridge takes something out of me. Elizabeth and I came here when we first arrived in Florida. It was a new beginning for us, for Lilly and Evan as well. I remember standing here with them and looking out to the estuary. There was so much life around us; people were coming and going, and the river was full of boats. The sky was bright blue, like it is today, and Lilly and Evan had such a time feeding the seagulls. Everything seemed so fresh and promising. I never dreamed I would lose Elizabeth so soon, but as bad as that was, it was a natural part of life. Losing Lilly now, if in fact I have, is certainly an incomprehensible part of God's plan for me. But it may be part of his plan for me to use whatever talent I have to bring her back, and to right any other wrongs that have been committed along the way. I *have* to believe in Nick's innocence, and so do you. If he is found guilty, the real murderer will remain free, and no one will bother to find him. No one will bother to find Lilly. We will be alone in this. I will have lost my daughter; you will have lost your best friend; and that young man, who I know you care about, will have lost everything."

Grace didn't answer, but her pensive expression was enough for Judge Jenkins. He turned his thoughts inward, going over the facts again. He had been thinking all morning about Ivan and Mac. There were three people missing, he reasoned, and one of them killed Frank Moss. Lilly was the only sure victim. Ivan was a possible victim, and Mac was—well, everything about Mac was obscure, he thought. The only thing clear was the fact that he had created this whole, horrible nightmare.

The two continued with their walk in silence. Grace could hear the judge talking to himself under his breath, and then suddenly, he stopped and turned to her. "We have to concentrate on the motive. Mac would have the most logical motive for killing that man. His life was being threatened, no doubt, and he believed that the means to end the danger had been taken from him. I don't understand his motive for taking Lilly away, though. Could it be that he couldn't live here after what he had done, and he couldn't live without her?"

Grace shook her head. "I believe that he couldn't live without a woman," she answered decisively, "but I really don't think it would matter to him whether it was Lilly or somebody else. In fact, now that I think about it, he would probably rather have someone who doesn't know anything about him."

This concept was completely foreign to Lilly's father. He looked intently at Grace as she elaborated on the idea, and he could tell that she firmly believed every word she was saying. She had a different understanding of his daughter, he thought, and through that, a different understanding of Mac.

"So you don't believe she is with him now," he asked, although he already knew what her answer would be.

"As I told the police chief, I don't care about that old man being dead. I don't even really care if Nick killed him. I want Lilly to be safe. If she was kidnapped for revenge, that would be a horrible thing. If Mac killed Frank Moss, I have to hope he has Lilly. But what I hope and what I believe are two different things."

Chapter 23

Her head was pulled up by her hair and laid again on the pillow. For the first time, Lilly saw the man's face and tried to scream, but she started coughing again. Ivan tied a pillowcase over her mouth and tightly wrapped the folded bedspread around her body, tying the ends to the metal frame of the bed. He then walked outside the cottage and leaned against a tree. He lit a cigarette and decided to stand guard in the fresh air for a while, hoping to thwart any further visits from the nosy proprietor of the Sunshine Tourist Court.

Ivan was sure that someone would find the body of his father in a few hours. He was surprised that no one heard them screaming at each other. Perhaps they had. Anyone who had been unfortunate enough to occupy the same vicinity had surely become accustomed to the vitriolic explosions that emanated from their warehouse office. The latest incident was more than Ivan could stand. He had been proud of his success in tracking the woman down in Savannah. The money meant little to him; it was only important as a means of shutting up his father.

His idea about the baby had started off in a casual, off-hand way, but on the trip back to Tampa, it was all he could think about. Now, it was all he had. His father had thrown the bundle of money at him and told him he was as useless as tits on a bull. He told him his wife was probably in bed with a real man while he was chasing around the country for his money. Ivan answered in a way he never had before. His screams almost drowned out the shots from his revolver. He picked up some of the money, and on his way out of the warehouse, grabbed a can of the ether he had learned how to use. He spent most of the night sitting in his car behind the palmettos, going over in his mind the layout of Mac Harrison's house and the location of the bedroom where he knew he could find the mother of his new child.

His father was gone now. He was in charge of his own life, and he wasn't sorry. He would do things his own way and have things his own way.

Ivan smoked another cigarette and walked slowly back to the cottage. He could hear Lilly's labored breathing as soon as he opened the door. He pulled a chair close to the bed and held the small bedside lamp above her while he loosened the pillowcase around her face. While Lilly had been in the room alone, she had repeated constantly the same words: "please, please." She had addressed them to God; now she directed them to Ivan Moss.

Ivan sat down on the bed beside her before he answered. "I ain't gonna hurt you, lady. I just don't want you hurtin' me. I've had girls take a swing at me lots of times; sometimes they can land one pretty good. You just stay quiet and don't cause no trouble."

Lilly tried to talk above her pounding heart. "My father paid you—Nick gave you—I'm sure—I'm sure he gave you the money."

"Yeah, I know about the money. Why'd he give it to my old man? He coulda gave it to *me*. Your husband owed *me* the money; he was workin' for *me* when he stole it. Far as I'm concerned, he still owes me—*you* still owe me. We made a deal between us. I'll forget about everything else if you just have the baby like we agreed. You weren't supposed to come back. You were supposed to stay in Savannah and have it."

"Ivan, for God's sake, just work it out with your father."

"My father's got three bullets in his face. I shut his big, loud, stupid mouth for good."

Lilly pushed her feet against the bed, loosening the bedspread around her, and wriggled up to the head of the bed. The horror in her face took Ivan by surprise. He grabbed both her hands and tried to make her understand. "What are you worried about him for? He ain't nothin' to you. He ain't nothin' to nobody. I'm in charge of everything now. I'm gonna set myself up somewhere, and he can't do nothin' about it. You can come with me and see how a real man runs things. Your husband thought he was somethin' big, but he didn't know nothin'. He was just a fancy dancer. You ain't lost that much, losin' him. You come with me. You just come with me. I agreed to be the father of that baby, and when I make a deal with somebody, I come through on it. I'll show this kid everything I know. I won't be like my old man; I'll make somethin' of this kid. This'll be my kid. I'll do this thing right. You just come with me."

Lilly drew her knees up to her chin. The bedspread had become completely untied now and was draped loosely over her. With all her strength, and all the anger and rage inside her, she kicked out her legs. Both her heels struck Ivan squarely under the chin, moving his brain backward in his skull and cutting off, for a moment, the vital blood supply. He sank to the floor in a way he never had in the boxing ring. His arms fell to his side, and his body went limp. He swayed for a moment on his knees before falling back, unconscious, against the wall.

Lilly rolled off the other side of the bed and tried to stand up. The room turned, and she grabbed the window curtains as she started to fall, pulling the curtain rod down and sending a shaft of light out into the north Florida night.

Mr. Owens had looked up from his paper several times, glancing in the direction of the cottage across the lawn, and worrying about the lady whose husband seemed so unconcerned about her illness. When the impressive Cadillac had pulled in earlier that evening, there was no reason for suspicion. The man was well dressed but appeared tired from his trip. The woman sleeping against the passenger window was sick, he was told, but that was not an uncommon thing. The sight of the man carrying her through the cottage door had aroused his concern, however. She seemed limp, and her skin looked ashen, even from a distance. He had reluctantly retreated from her room after her husband had refused his help, but he had decided, without success, to put it out of his mind.

The sudden flash of light caused Mr. Owens to rise from his chair. He hurried to the cottage, determined this time to assess things more fully. Through the undraped window, he could see it all. The man was slumped against the wall, blood pouring from his lacerated lip, and the woman was lying on the floor, half covered by the curtains she was still clutching.

Chapter 24

Nick was pacing back and forth in his cell when Judge Jenkins came in to see him. He held up a finger to his lips to plead for silence until the guard walked away. "It's Ivan," Nick said excitedly. "I'm sure about it. This was a stupid thing, and Mac's not stupid. But Ivan is. A smart man knows when he's been beaten. I think that's exactly what happened to Mac. He lost, and he gave up. Ivan always went blindly after everything he wanted."

"Why would he kill his father, Nick?" said the judge, hoping that the answer would be convincing enough to end any remaining doubts that he had.

"I think a better question is how did he keep from doing it all these years? It was obvious to me, and to everyone who knew them, that Ivan hated his father. I've seen some violence in my life, but it was all cold-blooded. It's easier to shoot a man in the chest or the stomach. You have to hate someone to shoot them in the face like that. I kept thinking about that last night. I could see Ivan doing that. I could see it as plain as if I was there."

"That means that Ivan has Lilly, then."

"Yeah, Judge, it does. Ivan doesn't hate Lilly, though. He wants something from her. I think you should go home and wait. Try to convince the police to look for Ivan, but after that, go home and wait."

"To be honest with you, Nick, I really don't know what else to do, anyway. I don't know where to look for her. In the meantime, though, Ivan's absence makes him a much likelier suspect, and that should take some of the attention away from you. Everyone around here will understand that, no matter what Leland Davis thinks. Do you want me to send Grace in to see you?"

Nick thought a moment and then shook his head. "No, Judge, I don't think so. I don't want her to see me in here. I don't ever want her to see me in a place like this."

Those were the words that removed all lingering doubts in Judge Jenkins' mind. He shook Nick's hand and left in silence, feeling certain that he at least had found the truth.

The next morning, Judge Jenkins sat alone at his wife's heirloom cherry dining table. It had been a gathering place in joyful times before her death, the huge crystal punch bowl always presiding over the family festivities. Now, the widower bowed his head solemnly at the mostly bare table, delivering a prayer in his soft Georgia cadence, asking God to keep in his care the lives of these young people. He prayed first for his daughter but also for Evan and Grace and Nick. Their lives were entwined with Lilly's as much as his, he thought.

He ate only to strengthen himself for the battle in which he was engaged. The enemy was unseen, and the field was enormous and intimidating. His mood alternated between hope and despair. He had seen the outcome of passion and violence too many times. He had learned, also, that almost every attempt to allay danger was difficult and complex, that once harm threatened, it seemed to develop a life of its own. At the very moment it was about to be put down, it could turn and twist and assault you from another angle. But he felt that he knew Lilly better than anyone. He had seen the flash of heat in her eyes and the sudden coloring of her cheeks. He thought that if anyone could overcome an adversary, it would be her. He was sure, also, of the existence of an enemy; Lilly would never have left them to this.

He was suddenly aware of the sound of a motor. It was far off and faint, but as it grew, he became almost frozen. He wished for other faces at the table, other eyes to search for confirmation—and for hope. He stood up, his heart pounding, as the car engine revved up at the gate to take on the soft sand, which was now turning muddy from the morning rain.

Grace and Evan were out of the Model T by the time he reached the porch. Dr. Morgan slammed the car door and hurried to catch up. Lilly's father looked frantically at their faces, and he could see through the dripping rain that they were all smiling. Grace spoke first. "They've got her! They've got her! The police in Jacksonville just called us; they say she's in the chief's office up there. She's O.K. An officer will be bringing her home by tonight."

Judge Jenkins nearly collapsed from the shock of initial fear and then overwhelming relief, but he was forced to recover when Grace almost leapt into his arms.

Dr. Morgan pulled her away to deliver the rest of the news. "It was Moss, Judge. It was that damned hoodlum. He confessed to killing his father after they brought him around. He was out for a time, I was told. Lilly apparently knocked him out and put two of his teeth through his lip."

Everyone but Lilly's father laughed.

Chapter 25

The lingering rain of that October morning had drifted across Florida ahead of a blast of cold air, removing all traces of the recent boiling summer. Throughout the afternoon, the early northern wind whistled in the gray cypress trees and rattled the wooden frames of the window screens.

Judge Jenkins lit the first fire of the season in the front parlor and wearily sat down beside his son to wait for Lilly's arrival. "We've lost a lot," he began, "everything I worked for, everything I saved for you and Lilly. It doesn't mean a damned thing, Evan. If I had kept all that and lost your sister, I would have nothing. I know she's upset about losing the money I gave her, but lately I've wondered if I gave it to her for the right reasons. Was I just trying to make myself look larger? I think of all the things your mother and I accumulated over the years. What is it all for? It'll be gone someday—it'll belong, in all likelihood, to someone who never knew that we walked on this earth. Don't ever forget that, Son. I want you to be successful, but don't be driven by material possessions. I don't want you to wake up one morning, like I did, and find that it's too late to make up for your shortcomings. I would give anything to have a few more days with your mother. I was so enslaved to that office in town that I lost sight of everything else. What is that to me now? Those people forgot about me as soon as I walked out the door. I suspect the people in Savannah did the same. When Lilly gets home, tell her you love her. Nothing else is worth a damned thing, Son. Not a damned thing."

It was well after midnight when the southbound train chugged noisily into the Calusa Depot. The deputy thanked the officer from Jacksonville and helped Lilly to his car. She had gotten some sleep on the train and was feeling surprisingly well. The deputy had never spoken to her before, but knew who she was. He tried to keep her company during the dark ride without needlessly prying into her troubles. "It's wonderful to have you home safe, Mrs. Harrison," he began. "There were plenty of folks worried about you. A reporter from the paper was hanging around the depot till almost midnight. I chased him home. Those guys get under my skin like nothing in the world."

"What story would he write, I wonder?" said Lilly, talking, it seemed, to herself more than to the man beside her. "A man is dead; another is going to be hanged; another is ruined and lost. Would the readers be sorry for me? Ivan Moss did a terrible thing, but you know, at one point in my life, I was going to do a terrible thing to my baby. It would have been torn from its resting place for no other reason than that I couldn't find a place in my life for it. It would not have had the chance that I had. It would not have had the strength that I had, but it would have kicked as I did, I'm sure. Getting rid of this child would have been a heartless, cowardly thing to do. I'm not like that—I'm strong, and I can rise above my fears. Ivan Moss's life was a brutal, hellish thing, but he found a place in it for this baby. He evidently wanted, in his own twisted way, something to love. People will think I gained my freedom by striking Ivan when I did, but the truth is, I was already free. And all that money—all that money that came and went so fast—couldn't buy my freedom, but the baby did. Let them write *that* story— that an unwanted, unborn child was my ransom."

Epilogue

Winter was Lilly's favorite season. There was a real Thanksgiving to start it off that year. She had many reasons to be thankful, and so did her papa. His son was home, and even without the benefit of law school, Evan was proving to be an excellent partner. Judge Jenkins had finally become comfortable in the house again. He was able to think of Elizabeth in ways that didn't evoke a sense of sorrow and loss.

Lilly also enjoyed the company of her brother. They felt like children again as they decorated the Christmas tree and set off fireworks on New Year's Eve. Everyone's favorite entertainment was badgering Nick and Grace to get married. Nick had finally bought his orange grove, and Grace had surprised everyone by her talent as a grower. She looked as much at home on the tractor as she did in the Model T.

Lilly thought they were perfect for each other. Nick wasn't the least bit intimidated by Grace's modern flapper style, and his kind, patient manner and easy good humor

were just what she needed. There was a goodness about
Nick that everybody noticed. Lilly was glad that he had
changed the course of his life, and she could think of
no better reward for anybody than the love of her best
friend.

By April, everyone was anxious for the arrival of
Lilly's baby. They all knew about the ether. Dr. Morgan
maintained his optimism and tried to pass it on to
everybody else. The delivery was agonizingly long
and difficult, but the baby was beautiful. Lilly named
her Naomi, not because it had been a family name in
Georgia, but because of its Hebrew meaning: my delight.
Naomi cried and moved as healthily as all babies should.
She nursed heartily and grew before their very eyes.

Life continued to unfold in a normal way. The
decision to open the small law practice had proven
to be a good one. Clients began to come every day. A
surprising number were women whose husbands had
died after coming home from the war. Judge Jenkins and
Evan helped them with their petitions for relief.

A young woman holding a baby at the front door
one afternoon was probably one of these widows, Lilly
thought, as she opened the door and ushered her into the
parlor. The woman smiled nervously and asked to see
Evan.

"I'm sorry; he's away just now," said Lilly.

"Are you Mrs. Jenkins?"

"I'm not Mrs. Evan Jenkins; I was *Miss* Jenkins for
most of my life. Evan is my brother. My name is Lilly
Harrison."

"Oh, I was almost sure you were. I expected to find
that Evan had a wife, and you are just what I pictured she

would look like. I'm wrong then, I suppose, unless there is another woman here who *is* his wife."

Lilly almost answered out of politeness, but the strangeness of the young lady's question, and the inappropriate tone in which it was delivered, made her stop. "I'm sorry, ma'am, I neglected to ask your name."

"My name is Emily—Emily Creighton."

"I'm pleased to meet you, Mrs. Creighton. Do you know my brother well?"

It's *Miss* Creighton. We met in New Orleans—excuse me—in Pensacola when he came there to see a client last summer."

Lilly's suspicion grew as she searched her mind for anything that would relate to the woman's statement. Her father overheard the words as he came out of his office. "I'm Robert Jenkins—Evan's father," he said. "I'm sorry, I just heard you say that you had met him in Pensacola. You may have him confused with an old partner of mine from another law firm. I haven't sent Evan on any errands of that nature."

"He said he worked for his father," Emily answered defensively.

The mild confusion that Lilly and her father felt was beginning to grow into discomfort when they heard Evan's car coming up to the house. They waited in awkward silence for Evan to walk into the room. When he finally did, the total absence of any look of recognition on his face, or on the face of the young woman, puzzled them even more. Emily wasted no time in adding to the mystery. "You're not Evan. The Evan Jenkins I met was older. He was probably twenty-five or so. He was taller. I think my baby—his baby——looks like him, but it just may be my imagination. I wanted to find him because he changed my life. I know that he didn't mean to, but what he did changed me. What he did made me stop what I was doing, and then the baby saved me. The baby was my redemption."

Lilly had taken little notice of the mention of New Orleans, but it suddenly sent a shock through her mind. She quickly left the room without excusing herself and went to the bedroom to look for her wedding picture. She found it at the bottom of a drawer, turned face down beneath some folded clothes. It had been one of her favorite pictures. She thought she looked pretty, and everybody always commented about the groom. "Captain Harrison is a fine man," they all said.

About The Author

Ensley Williams is a native of Tampa, where he received a B.A. in anthropology from the University of South Florida. *Lilly's Ransom* is his first novel. Much of his inspiration for the book, especially the Gullah dialogue in Chapter 14, comes from the writings of his great-grandfather, Rev. John G. Williams. In the late nineteenth century, *Coteny Sermons* first appeared in serial form in the *Weekly News and Courier* (Charleston, S.C.), and later as a volume published by Walker, Evans & Cogswell Company. Ensley Williams is currently revising the collection of Gullah sermons and plans to release it in the fall of 2006.